MoonChild

Lena Armstrong

Contents

1. The Move

I should be used to this. I should be used to moving all the time. I guess in a way, I was. I was just growing tired of it. My dad was a US Ambassador so we'd been nearly everywhere. Germany, Great Britain, Italy, Japan, and even Syria for a time before it got really bad there. The last place we lived was Australia. It was my favorite. It was also the longest we stayed in one place: three years. I almost made it all the way through high school, but of course, with my luck, we moved just in time for my senior year. My dad personally picked this one and it was a little odd... Virginia. It was only odd because it was home for my father. It was where he grew up.

It was just me and my father. My mother died in a car accident when I was a preteen. I didn't miss her though. I actually despised the woman. If I didn't do something exactly the way she wanted, I got strips of leather against my back or some other form of torture. I don't miss it at all, but I still have the scars to prove it.

Our new house was huge, but they all were. They were embassies for ambassadors with diplomatic immunity and loads of security. The security got old really fast. I had at least two on me everywhere I went, if not more. The sketchier the country, the more security followed me around.

"So what do you think?" he asked nervously. To be honest, I hadn't really been paying much attention. My father and I weren't alike at all. He loved adventure and seeing new things, and I was content being in my room, listening to music, and reading a good book. We didn't look anything alike either. In fact, I didn't look like either of my parents. My mother, before she died, had copper red hair, a narrow face, tan skin, and soulless brown eyes. She was tall and thin and beautiful. My father was more of a free spirit. Although his spirit grew weaker after my mother died. He had dirty blonde hair, a square face, and warm, brown eyes. Compared to them, I was sure I was adopted. I had jet black hair that was thick and slightly curly, unlike my parents' straight hair. My eyes were silver, almost eerily. My face was heart-shaped, I had dimples, and my skin was almost translucent, I was so pale.

I looked at the house; really looked at it. Every embassy had the same structure and setup in every country... except this one. It was made primarily of red brick that was darker and lighter in spots due to age and weather. There was a roundabout in front of the house with a water fountain in the middle. There was a set of white double doors and windows lined the front of the house like giant soldiers. The top of the house had the typical American dark paneling on angled roofs that pierced the sky at different heights. Thick trees lined both sides of the house. I didn't see any concrete walls or watch towers. This wasn't an embassy at all. My face scrunched in confusion as I looked to my father.

"What's going on?" I asked, knowing immediately that something was wrong with this picture. Ambassadors didn't do stations inside the states, and this wasn't a secure building. I knew he'd already shipped most of my stuff here, but where was here exactly?

"I know you're tired of moving all the time, and you're almost 18 years old now, so... you're not going with me to my next station. You're not going to a private school either. You're going to live with your grandparents here, and go to the local school. My next station isn't here, but you place is," he tried to explain.

"So what? You're just... dropping me off with grandparents I've never met before, in a place I don't know and you're just telling me this now... in front of their house?" I asked, my voice rising with every word. I had a tendency to talk faster, louder and higher the more upset I got, and this was one of those times. My blood was boiling and I knew my face was red with anger. For the majority of my life, it'd just been us. Yes, we were different, but my father was my rock. He was my best friend. He was the only one I relied on to be there for me, and he was just leaving me behind. I felt betrayed.

"I'm sorry. I tried to tell you, but I just... I couldn't. It kills me, not being able to take you with me. But you can't go where I'm going. I made a deal with your mother. I promised her that you would be here when you turned 18, and it's that time. Patrick and Nora Wilders, your mother's parents," he explained with his head hung and shoulders hunched. I still felt like he wasn't telling me everything.

"No! No way. I'm not staying with the people who raised the devil herself," I argued, crossing my arms. He growled lowly at me in warning. He did that often when I stepped out of line, but it didn't really affect me this time. I wasn't going through this again. I wasn't going to stand for it. I wasn't going to live with the people who created my nightmare. My father sighed heavily; his façade falling away with the breath. He looked tired and old in this moment. Like he'd been putting on a face for my sake but he couldn't keep it up anymore. His face looked paler and wrinkled. He looked older than he was. He was worn down.

"Not Evelyn... you're real mother, Rebecca," he admitted hesitantly. My mouth hung open slightly in shock. I felt my body go cold with shock. My nightmare, the woman who tortured me endlessly, the woman I tried to get the approval of, the woman I tried to please, the woman I called my mother, was an imposter.

"You just let me believe she was my mother," I breathed as tears stung my eyes. "She tortured me endlessly and you did nothing! And you want to drop a bomb like this as you're dropping me off at my unknown mother's parent's house? Now? Really?" I yelled at him as my anger melted my shock.

"I know, and I'm sorry, but there was a reason for everything. Evelyn was a necessary evil. I know you hate me for this right now, but you'll understand eventually; in due time," he said quickly, finally looking at me with glossy eyes and guilt riddled all over his face. A couple appeared on the porch, watching us; waiting for me. I looked just like them. The woman, who I assumed was Nora Wilders, my grandmother, had the same dark thick hair and dimples. She was dressed in a blue sweater and jeans. The man, Patrick Wilders, my grandfather, was in a button up, plaid shirt and jeans. From this far, I calculated that they looked too young to be grandparents.

"I loved your mother more than you could ever know. She was my soul and my heart, and I made her a promise. I took care of you as best as I could without her. I know you don't understand what Evelyn did. I know it was cruel for a child, but you survived. You owe your life to her. I know you don't understand now, but you will soon," he said as his tears finally fell. I felt the feeling of defeat coming off of him in waves. The man who raised me gave off the impression of being full of life and adventure, but this man before me now was different. Now that the kid goggles were off, I could see that he was hollow and broken inside. My dad always said I was an empath. I could easily sense the mood of others around me. And all I felt from him at the moment was emptiness and guilt. I tried to sympathize. I tried to see it from his side, but I couldn't get over my own feeling of betrayal.

"You lied to me my whole life," I accused him in a calm tone as tears rolled down my face. He was only an inch away from sobbing himself. The car felt too small, too confined, too sad. "Maybe it's best to get some space from you right now anyway," I said as I pushed the car door open. The air held a brisk nip that I wasn't ready for. My short sleeved shirt and jeans felt paper thin as the wind ruffled my hair. I wiped the now cold tears from my face before going to grab all two of my bags from the trunk. With us always moving, I learned how to pack light. Plus, the rest of my things were already here, probably in a closet somewhere.

"Dani!" my father begged as he got out as well. I ignored him as I started towards the couple who was still watching us.

"I'll see you whenever you decide to come back," I threw over my shoulder as I decided that I'd be better off without him.

2. A Start of Sorts

The woman smiled softly before she hugged me tightly. The gesture was heartfelt and meaningful; like a prodigal child was returning. I guess to them, that was exactly what was happening. I felt her love and sympathy leaking through her. I dropped my bags on the ground and hugged her back, craving the comfort and warmth I so desperately needed at the moment.

"Oh Daniella... I know you don't know us yet, but we're going to change that. We haven't seen you since you were a newborn," the woman blubbered. I could feel her tears against my cheek. Her body heat radiated off of her in a calming way. It protected me from the chilling wind.

"Nora, the child is probably cold," Patrick said. Nora sniffled before she let go and brought me inside. Patrick picked up my bags and set them inside the door before going back outside. Probably to talk to my father. Nora rushed me into the house and sat me down on a plush brown couch before sitting on the coffee table in front of me and rasping my hand in her own. Being this close, I noticed her eyes were a sky blue with flecks of silver. The same silver that consumed the whole of my irises. At least now I could see where it might have come from.

She didn't say anything. She just sat there, holding my hand tightly and staring at me like I could disappear at any moment. I could feel every emotion she felt. It hit me like a wave at high tide. Her eyes intense and focused on every feature I possessed; comparing them to my mother's.

My concentration broke and I jumped when the door slammed. Patrick came into the room and saw us just sitting there. Nora's eyes were still on me as I looked at Patrick. He looked sympathetically to his wife as he released her iron grasp on my hand, breaking her emotions from me.

"Love, you're scaring the poor girl," Patrick said as he took my hand and placed it gently on my own lap before letting go. He smiled warmly at me. His eyes were a green color with flecks of gold. Patrick's hair was brown, but graying slightly. His skin looked like he was in the sun often.

"I'm sorry! Did you want tea, or soup, or hot chocolate, or water, or anything?" Nora asked as she stood quickly. I shook my head. I looked between the two of them and offered a small awkward smile.

"At least I know where my looks come from finally," I said, trying to break the awkward silence with a shrug. Nora's face lit up as she went to retrieve something. Patrick squeezed my shoulder gently as Nora came back with a picture frame. She looked at it was a face of sadness and love for a moment before she turned it for me to see.

"Rebecca Grace... She was your mother," Nora said, handing me the picture. The wood of the frame was old but well taken care of. In the frame was my father and what I knew now was my real mother. My mom was draped over the back of my father as they smiled at the camera. Her black hair shined with a dark brown undertone brought out by the sun's rays. Her heart-shaped face held a wide smile of her full, pink lips, showing off her one dimple. The slits of her eyes hinted at a blue or gray iris. The crinkles on the side of her eyes suggested that she was laughing. Her sun-kissed, porcelain-like skin was flawless as she wore a white sundress. She was stunningly beautiful.

My father looked like a completely different person. He looked completely in love like I'd never seen him before. He looked happy... truly happy. I think this was the first time I'd ever seen his smile reach his eyes. He put on a good act, but as I got older, I started noticing it more and more. I started noticing how sad he really was. Maybe I was too hard on him. He did have to raise me by himself. But he kept my real mother a secret from me, and I was still very upset about that.

"She's so beautiful," I said out loud.

"And you look just like her," Nora said. I smiled lightly, content that I at least knew where my looks came from now.

"She passed away in child birth, but she made your father promise to take care of you and bring you back here before you turned 18. You were everything to your mother. She chose your life over her own," Nora said solemnly. I could tell that they loved me mother very much, and missed her greatly. I felt guilty for being the one who ripped her away from them. No parent should have to deal with the pain of outliving their child.

"Come on, we'll give you a tour of the house and then you can get some rest. You already missed the first few months of school here, but we en-rolled you in Roosevelt. It's the local high school. Everyone from our quiet little town goes there. And our family has been going there for genera-tions," Patrick said as he stood. I had to admit, I was a little nervous. Being an Ambassador's daughter, I never actually went to a public school. I was always going to private institutions with other ambassador's kids and kids of CIA operatives and whatnot. Public school would be new to me. I handed the picture frame back to Nora and stood to follow Patrick around the house.

The house was big as far as regular homes go. It was warm and welcoming though. I didn't feel out of place or foreign. I felt right at home. We ended the tour at my room. The walls were painted a dark blue. The room was spacious with cherry wood furniture. The bed sat against the middle of the wall on the left. The duvet was a portrait of two wolves on the edge of a cliff, howling at a full moon. It was artistically beautiful. There was so much detail; it looked so real.

"W-We can always change it if you want," Nora offered nervously. They were both nervous about making me feel welcome, I noticed. I smiled at them reassuringly.

"It's perfect," I assured them. It was the truth though. I loved everything about this room. And the wolf theme was different and unique and beautiful.

"You're mother loved that blanket. She took the picture herself. She loved it so much we had it made into a blanket for her 18th birthday," Nora said, deep in thought. My eyebrows raised in surprise. The picture was so perfect it was almost unreal. It was amazing. There was so much about her I didn't know. So much I wanted to know.

"Bathroom?" I asked.

"Through that door there," Patrick pointed out a door inside the room.

"Dinner will be ready in 15 minutes if you're hungry," Nora added. I thanked them before they left me alone to settle my things. I sighed and checked my phone. I had two texts. The first was from my friend Jannah.

Jannah: Miss you boo! You better text me updates and FaceTime me tomorrow! ;)

I chuckled silently to myself as I shook my head at my crazy friend. With super curly brown hair, caramel skin, mischievous brown eyes, and a body to die for, Jannah was the only friend I made that I knew would stick. She lived in Australia when I did. She was the daughter of the Ambassador of Brazil. There was a lot of space between us, but I had a feeling that it wouldn't restrict our friendship much. The second text made me frown in worry. It was from my dad.

Dad: I'm so sorry Dani girl. I was only trying to protect you. I love you.

It sounded eerily like a goodbye that meant he wasn't coming back and I hated that feeling. I called and it went straight to voicemail. Even though I was mad at him, I still loved and cared about him. He was my dad after all. I was just upset that he lied to me. After trying to call him two more times, I settled for sending him a text.

Me: I love you too, Dad.

I pulled my clothes out of my bags, put them in drawers and hung them in the closet. The rest of my things were already neatly in place. I set my toiletries in the bathroom before finding a soft, plush towel and setting it aside for a shower. I liked it here so far. My grandparents were loving and kind, but tears still blended with the water as the hot water assaulted my body. I sighed and tried to calm my trembling body. Once my body was heated and scrubbed, I stepped out and dried myself off before changing into a long sleeved shirt and pants pajama combo.

I climbed under the covers that used to be my mother's. It smelled like lilac and lemons. It was a mild but beautiful smell. I wondered if it was how my mother used to smell. I liked to think so. It made me feel like I could have known her. She was probably a kind and caring person like her parents were. I smiled gently and closed my eyes with every intention of taking a short nap before dinner.

3. Preminition

"Daniella... Daniella, wake up, you're going to be late for school," Nora's gentle voice traveled to my ears. I shot up with a short gasp. I'd been tossing and turning all night with nightmares. I dreamed of my father driving his car straight off a cliff and into a river. It was like I was there with him. It was like I was him. I felt his depression, his sadness, his anxiety and guilt. I felt the moment when he decided that he'd done his job and kept his promise and life wasn't worth living anymore without his true love. I felt his loneliness. I saw him veer the car into the freezing river. I watched as the car fell under the light layer of ice and stated to fill with water. I felt him inhale the water and accept his death. As things started blacking, he was content. He wanted to be with my mother... his soulmate.

I relived the dream over and over until Nora woke me. It was painful to watch and feel. I didn't even realize I was crying. My shaking breath and runny nose provoked me to touch my cheek and feel the tears. My new room slowly came into focus.

"Are you alright, dear?" Nora asked me, worried. Her gaze was focused in on my eyes as she stared at me in wonder and worry. She was rubbing my back in a comforting manner. I sighed and buried my face in my hands for a brief moment.

"I just had this nightmare about my dad," I admitted when I finally looked at her. I told her all of it. By the end, I was in tears again. She rested my head on her chest as she rubbed my back.

"I'm so sorry, Dani. I know that your mother's passing was the hardest on you father. After your mother passed, he disappeared with you, but as you can see, he kept his promise. Losing a soulmate can make someone lose the will to live," she sympathized. I was confused and more scared than before.

"But it was just a dream... right?" I asked. She nodded.

"Of course, sweetheart. No one can know the future. Maybe you were subconsciously picking up on your father's mood and your brain created a worst case scenario," she said before she stood with a sigh. "The school is only a fifteen minute walk normally, but I'll drive you since it's winter and the temperature is only going drop, I'll drive you until it gets warmer. Dress warmly," Nora said, changing the subject before she left my room quickly. I was sensing a major diversion there, but I let it go and got up to get ready. I didn't want to be late to my first day of school.

I quickly got dressed in a red sweater and jeans with a leather jacket and gray scarf. I left my hair down for fear of making my ears beat red and on display. My pale skin made it really easy to see where my blood was flowing to. I tried tanning and makeup but it was too much effort, and half the time I would just burn a brighter red. I didn't bother with makeup. My long, thick eyelashes were pitch black, standing out just fine on their own without any extra help. My cheeks turned red if the wind blew the wrong way. And my semi-full lips were always pink. Chapstick was all I used. It saved a lot of time.

I jogged down the stairs and helped myself to the breakfast Nora prepared. Eggs and bacon on bagels. I skipped on the eggs and bacon though because I was a vegetarian. I spread cream cheese on a bagel and opted for some of the oatmeal sitting on the stove. Patrick watched my choices with confusion.

"You don't want any bacon or eggs? I picked it up fresh last night. A friend of mine owns a farm not too far from here. It's all fresh," Patrick asked. I blushed, feeling rude for not acknowledging the effort.

"I'm actually a vegetarian. I don't eat meat," I answered. He chuckled and shook his head as he walked away.

"Not yet anyway," he muttered under his breath. It didn't sound like it was meant for my ears but I heard it anyway. I ignored his weird comment and ate quickly before Nora fetched me for school. We walked outside and into the crisp air. I was glad I grabbed the extra jacket. No doubt the cold turned my face pink. We got in her beat up, gray pickup truck and headed down the cracked and worn asphalt road.

"I think you'll like the school. It's full of good kids. I heard you tell Pat that you were a vegetarian this morning," Nora admitted. I nodded sheepishly.

"I have been since I was nine years old," I said for sake of conversation. When people normally asked, I always said it was a personal choice based on a documentary I watched, or something along those lines. It was easier than trying to explain the real reason. It was easier than saying it was because Evelyn used to tie me up, make me watch as she beheaded a chicken and barely cooked it. By the time she was done "cooking", my face would be red and blotchy from crying over the bloodshed. Then, she force-fed me the meal, every bite, until I was so full that I would throw up the partially raw meat. She would then, re-feed it to me until every bite was kept down.

"I packed you a lunch, but it was a ham sandwich, so here's some money to buy your own lunch. It's the best I could do with a last minute's notice," Nora apologized as she held out a twenty. I felt bad. She was trying her best to make me feel at home and I wasn't making it that easy.

Looking around, I saw the truck was parked in the front of a very old but huge building. Kids from 14 to 19 years old were hanging around, knowing exactly where to go and when. Something I would have to get used to all over again. I reached over and pulled her into a hug as I released a breath. I felt her love for me rolling off of her and reveled in it.

"Thanks grandma," I said softly. I heard her small gasp before she held onto me even tighter. When I pulled away, I saw the tears she was trying to hold back. She looked happy; like it was something she had been waiting to hear. She held a smile as she touched my cheek gently for a moment.

"Great, now you're going to make me start blubbering," she chuckled as she tried to dry her eyes. "Go; you're going to be late for school," she sniffed as her hand fell away from her face. I took the money she offered me and stepped out of the heated cab of the truck and into the cold. I pulled my jacket around myself a little tighter as I headed towards the unknown that was my new school. My new life.

4. Intentions

I walked quickly into the school and kept my head down to ignore the obvious stares I was getting. Luckily, the front office was the first thing I ran into. I stepped inside quickly before shedding my jacket in the heated building. I looked to the woman at the front counter awkwardly; unsure of how to approach her. Luckily, she sensed my presence and looked up with a friendly smile.

"Hi, how can I help you?" she asked warmly.

"I-I'm new... Daniella Morison?" I answered unsurely. You'd think I'd be used to starting over by now, but the awkwardness never wavered. I was still the awkward, timid, and unsure girl that Evelyn made me to be. I hated meeting new people. I always seemed to know their true intentions before they even opened their mouth. Another curse of being an empath. I was getting nostalgia and pity from the woman behind the counter for some reason as she looked at me.

She looks just like her mother.

It wasn't my thought; it was hers. I had imagined someone's thoughts before every once in a while, but it was more like a feeling. It was weak, but it had been happening more and more lately. I was probably just losing it. There was no way I could read people's thoughts. My imagination was getting out of control.

The woman typed on the keyboard in front of her, glancing up every once in a while to look at me curiously and sympathetically. After an awkward moment of the typing being the only noise inside the office, she handed me a schedule.

"Here you go. I'm Mrs. Carson, by the way. I'll call for an office aid to help you get around for today so you won't get lost," she offered. I thanked her quietly before she disappeared behind a door behind the counter. I stood there by myself awkwardly until she came back with someone in tow.

The girl was tall and thin. Her skin was perfectly sun kissed. Her chocolate brown hair hung in long, loose waves that faded to blonde. Her hazel brown eyes sparkled with mock happiness. I was momentarily confused on if she was walking towards me or down a runway. Her cropped jeans with ankle boots and pink blouse with an open cream blazer layered over it only solidified my model theory. With her in the room, I felt very small, plain, and insignificant. She flashed her pearly, straight, white teeth at me and held her hand out to me.

"You must be Daniella. I'm Sophia," she introduced herself. I shook her hand and gasped with the contact. Her hand was hot compared to my icy digits, but what took my breath away was the image I saw when her skin touched mine. My vision faded to black before a different, foggier picture appeared. It was Sophia, but her canine teeth were elongated. Her eyes glowed with anger as a growl ripped through her throat. It was like something out of Twilight. Although there were no imagined thoughts, the message and feeling were clear: she saw me as her competition in this school. Someone to embarrass, get rid of, or isolate.

I released my hand from hers quickly as I took a step back. I still couldn't see anything but black, but it was slowly starting to fade back to normal with the exception of a fog around reality. Mrs. Carson and Sophia were staring at me in a sense of wonder, confusion, and fear. They were staring directly at my eyes. I could feel my cheeks and neck heat under their stares.

"Your eyes," Sophia breathed in disbelief. I turned and stumbled out of the office and into the nearest bathroom with my schedule in hand. The fog didn't let up on my vision as I went to look at myself in the mirror. My head ached slightly but nothing too major. The girl in the mirror was a replica of me, except her face was flushed red and her eyes had no pupil the vision of haze. The eyes only reflected a glowing full moon. All the way down to the darker gray areas that held the moon's craters.

I didn't understand. I wasn't sure what was happening to me, but I didn't like it. I'd never seen a person's intentions in a literal vision before. I'd never seen them so clearly and in pictures. I took a few deep breaths and splashed a little water on my face before staring at the girl in the mirror again. The leftover haze faded, turning my moon-like irises back to their abnormal silver color. One thing was certain though: it happened when I touched Sophia.

I stepped out of the bathroom with the intention to find everything on my own after the front office fiasco. I did not want to be noticed at this school. With only one year left, it was my goal to go on invisible. Which inevitably meant that I had to stay the hell away from Sophia. She wanted to embarrass and destroy me. With one look, her mind was made up, and with one touch, so was mine. I looked down the empty hallways and went in the direction I was pulled to hesitantly. I normally trusted my instincts, but after this morning, I was a little cautious. This town was screwing with me. I could always find my locker and ask someone for help later.

After walking down a few hallways, I found the first door that matched the first block on my schedule. Knowing all eyes were going to be on my late entry, I pulled my hair around my face to hide it before taking a deep breath and pushing the door open. The teacher's hand froze in mid-air with a marker in his hand as his eyes diverted to me.

"Ah, Miss Daniella. I've been expecting you. I'm Mr. Willis. Take any open seat," he said before turning back to writing on the white board. It was history... first thing in the morning...

Just perfect.

I turned to the class to look for an open seat. I saw the looks of wonder and curiosity. I was getting a lot of feelings from a lot of people. I kept my head down and took the open seat in the very back. I pushed my hair further in a curtain around my face and stared at my desk while keeping an ear on Mr. Willis' lesson.

"Lilac, sea breeze, and lemon," the guy next to me muttered to himself as he inhaled deeply.

"Excuse me?" I asked quietly as I peeked over to look at him. He was already looking at me. His eyes held mine. Warm amber irises damn near took my breath away. My eyes moved to the rest of his face. His smooth brown hair, his sharp cheekbones, straight nose, soft-looking pink lips, strong jawline, long eyelashes, clear sun touched skin...everything.

"You're beautiful," he breathed as he stared on, stuck under whatever spell I was unknowingly casting on him. He blinked in realization as a faint blush touched his cheeks. He turned away from me and faced forward again. He looked confused as he blinked at his desk. I wanted to know his intentions as clear as I saw Sophia's, but I didn't' want to risk being a pariah on my first day. I had the strongest urge to touch him. I shook my head slightly to snap out of it and faced forward; trying to ignore the stranger beside me.

As soon as the bell rung, I shot up to leave. The sooner I got out in front, the more of a chance everyone would just see my back. The guy next to me grabbed onto my arm to stop me, but his hand slipped down my sleeve and touched the skin of my hand. He held onto it; skin on skin. I gasped as my vision went black like it did in the front office. Before it got too out of control, I closed my eyes, not wanting to draw attention to myself in case my eyes changed again. I tried to tug my hand out of his but it was no use.

"I just want to talk to you," his voice faded from my hearing. The new picture faded into my vision like a movie.

It was him. He was laying with me under a canopy tree in the middle of the forest. We had a picnic blanket underneath us in the sunset. The back of his finger stroked my cheek, sending chills all over my body. I couldn't help but smile at him. He kissed me gently. His lips were soft but eager. The kiss filled me with love and lust. He cared for me. The smell of pine and mint leaves surrounded me; causing me to relax. It was coming from him.

"I love you, Dani. We're meant to be together, you know that," he smiled at me adoringly. The vision version of myself smiled back at him as her hand ran through his hair and she nodded.

"I love you too, Liam," she said, and she meant it with all of her heart. She was drawn to him; made for him. She felt closer to him than anyone else in her entire life. His hand trailed down and pierced through her chest, wrapping his fingers around her literal heart. She gasped with shock as it felt like she had the wind knocked out of her as she stared at her love. He watched confused at her brokenness.

"I never meant for this to happen," he whispered sympathetically at the pain he could have prevented. He ripped her heart from her chest and stood with it as he squeezed it tighter between his fingers. Sophia appeared and pulled him away as she lay there bleeding with her heart still in Liam's possession. He took it with him, as he laced his other hand with Sophia's and walked away from her. He felt bad, but not bad enough to fix it. I gasped as the vision ended and I was thrown back into reality. My vision going back to black.

The guy, that I now knew was named Liam, still had his hand on mine. I knew his curiosity and interest and understood what he would do; consciously or not. He would love me. We would love each other, but he would unknowingly, and maybe even accidentally, hurt me emotionally. I opened my eyes to look at him, only to realize my vision was still fogged. He was stunned immediately.

"Your eyes," he breathed. My eyes... I forgot about the moon-like eyes. I turned away from him quickly and blinked while rubbing my eyes until the fog went away completely. I blinked a few times, to readjust my sight. It felt like I was in the beginning stages of a migraine.

"You-"

"Stay away from me, Liam. I'm serious," I said. He was confused.

"I never told you my name," he noted. Crap; he was right. I broke my hand from his grasp while he was distracted. I had no excuse for knowing his name, and telling him that my vision told me was just crazy. I shook my head slightly before I rushed out of the classroom. These visions were getting out of control. I felt, in my gut, that there was truth in what I was seeing. I didn't know what they meant just yet, but I knew that one felt too real to risk letting it come true. I had to be more careful. If what I was seeing was real, or even an exaggerated version of what was to come, it wouldn't help my low profile at all. And the headaches that accompanied them weren't too pleasant either.

5. Just Lunch

I released a breath when I was safely hidden in the crowd. I paid attention to the locker numbers and found the pattern leading to my own locker. Glancing at the paper, I unlocked the lock attached to the metal rings holding the locker shut with shaking hands. I opened it to find a blank canvas of a locker. The blue paint was chipping and the rust collected in the corners and on the shelves. I felt a little sily when I realized that I had nothing to put in the locker except my jacket and scarf, but I figured I could stare at the blank space until my hands stopped shaking at least. I stared at it another moment before I felt a tap on my clothed shoulder. I still jumped back slightly anyway.

"Staring isn't going to make anything appear," a feminine voice said from behind me. I turned to see a girl. She had thick, straight, reddish brown hair and hazel green eyes. Her cheeks were full on her round face. Her eyes were an open, almond shape. She was very pretty with a curvaceous figure that hid under draping clothing. She smiled warmly at me.

"I'm Mya," she said as she turned to open the locker next to mine. I could feel her intentions strongly from where I stood without touching her and, thankfully, without visions and episodes. She just wanted to be friendly to the new girl.

"I'm Dani... I have a feeling that this school doesn't get new people often," I said, making conversation to distract myself from my own problems. She chuckled and nodded as she switched her books out.

"A huge yes on that. Normally there's a whole process to even let an outsider join the pack, but everyone knows who you are. You look just like her," Mya said. I didn't quite know what to think of her words.

"Her?" I asked as I leaned against my closed locker and gave her my full attention.

"Rebecca Wilders. The former Beta's daughter. She was the most gifted healer the town ever had. They mourned her death for a long time. Her picture is still in the meet house," Mya explained nostalgically. I knew she couldn't have known my mother personally; she couldn't have been much older than me, but she talked about her like she did.

Beta? Healer? Pack? This town was starting to sound more like a cult than a town. I would have to remember to stay away from the water.

"Beta?" I picked out. Mya was still smiling until she looked at my confused face. Her smile dropped as she gave me her full attention.

"You didn't know your grandfather was a former beta?" she asked.

"I don't even know what a beta is," I answered in confusion. She looked shocked and stunned at the same time.

"Oh my God... have you even shifted yet?" she asked. This did nothing to help my confusion.

"Shifted?" I asked. She looked like she was about to pass out with how fast the blood drained from her face.

"You really have no idea," she breathed. She shook her head and turned back to her locker. "Forget I said anything," she muttered, trying to brush it off. My curiosity had already been sparked and I wanted to know what she was talking about. I wanted to get inside her mind. I was tempted to try touching her, but I wasn't even sure if that's how it worked.

I didn't even understand yet what this thing was or what I could possibly be exposing with my eyes. For all I knew, it could be dangerous. I would have to ask my grandparents when I got home. I smiled a little to myself, momentarily distracting myself with thoughts of my newfound grandparents. A lot of time was lost, but they seemed fully intent on making up for the lost time.

I felt his eyes on me before I actually saw him. When I turned, I saw them. Sophia was holding his hand as she laughed at something the friend next to her said. I couldn't hear anything; not even the regular noises of the hallway. I couldn't see anything anymore either as everything faded away except him. It wasn't like a vision, but more of a moment of infatuation as his eyes locked on mine. Sophia diverted his attention and the rest of the world came back into focus. I released a breath I didn't even know I was holding as I blinked hard and turned back to my locker to catch my breath. I felt slightly sick to my stomach.

"Whoa, what was that? You know A-Liam?" Mya asked.

"No," I answered a little too quickly.

"I wouldn't get in between those two if I were you. Liam and Sophia have been together since they were in elementary school," Mya warned.

"Trust me, I'm staying as far away from Liam as I can," I assured her quietly.

"What's your next class?" she asked, changing the subject. She leaned over to look at my schedule. "Math with Hamilton. You're in luck; I have that class right now, too. It's right down the hall," she said with a smile. She hooked her arm with mine and led me in the right direction. Mya seemed like a genuine person. She was my only friend here, at least for now. We entered the class and Mya sat me next to her in the middle of the classroom. The bell signaled the start of class.

After my math class, we had lunch. The school worked on an 'A-day', 'B-day' blocked schedule so the classes were an hour and a half long and I had different classes every other day. Thankfully, Mya invited me to sit with her at lunch. She walked with me to the cafeteria and led me through the line. I grabbed a Caesar salad before following Mya back to her table. A few of her friends were already sitting and talking with each other. Mya introduced everyone before we fell into comfortable chatter. I poured the dressing on generously before taking a bite. Mya eyed my food confused.

"You're not one of those health nuts, are you?" Mya asked jokingly. I chuckled and shook my head.

"I'm a vegetarian," I answered. Her friends at the table stared at me in confusion. What was with this town? It was like they never met a vegetarian before.

"I never thought I would see the day a wo-," Mya's friend, Kaden, started before he stopped abruptly to glare at Mya. She kneed him under the table before he could finish his sentence. Kaden was a simple soul; eat, sleep, repeat type.

"She doesn't know," Mya muttered so fast and so quietly that I almost missed it. I wanted so bad to know what she meant by that, but I felt frozen when I felt him. The hairs on the back of my neck pulled in his direction like a compass. I felt him approaching but I didn't dare turn around.

"Hey guys," Sophia's voice chimed. They sat at the same table across from me. Sophia smiled, touched Liam every once in a while, and held up a steady conversation with the table. She must have been a first lady in a past life. I tried to keep my eyes on my food as heat crept into my cheeks, but I could still feel his eyes on me. I hated the way I felt. I wanted to break every finger of hers that touched him. I had no idea where this possessiveness was coming from. It was unwarranted. It took me by surprise. I didn't even know Liam. I had guys I was friends with for a year ask me out and never felt this level of intimacy with them. And he only touched me once. I blamed my stupid hallucinations. Definitely drinking bottled water from here on out.

"Sweetie," Sophia said, turning his chin and taking his eyes off of me. I released a breath I didn't even know I was holding. "Did you hear me?" she asked him. Curiosity got the best of me and I peeked up just in time to see her move a strand of hair out of his face affectionately. I felt the urge to growl like my father would to me when I was getting out of line. It didn't make any sense.

Liam's eyes shot to mine. Those amber globes were full of guilt and conflict. He knew something was going on too. At least that was confirmation that I couldn't completely be making it up. I looked away first.

"So Daniella, the eye thing, have you always been that weird or is it a recent development?" Sophia asked, turning her attention to me. She didn't even try to hide her bitterness. She was leaned towards me with her chin resting on the palm of her hand and a smile painted on her face. By the way she looked and her tone, you would think she asked if I wanted to be her bridesmaid. The jealousy was coming off of her strongly, even from where I was sitting. But what did she have to be jealous of? The attention I was getting because I was the new girl? She could have it. I didn't want it anyway. Her intent was to destroy me. Right here... and right now.

"What eye thing?" I asked coolly, trying to play dumb.

"The thing where you wig our and your eyes turn into weird little moon replicas," she clarified. I took a bite of my salad as I tried to think of a lie.

"My eyes are naturally a silver color," I said, trying to shrug it off. But I honestly couldn't shrug off what I didn't understand myself.

"You naturally look like something out of the Twilight Zone?" she asked in mock innocence. Her impure undertones were easy to detect. She was trying to get a rise out of me and make me squirm.

"I have no idea what you're talking about," I said simply. She smiled sweetly and reached across the table.

"Don't' be shy, we're all friends here. I want to see it again," she said as she reached towards my skin. Liam stopped her hand as he growled lowly. It was kind of like my dad's was way more... primal. It was more of a warning that my dad ever gave me. His face was tinted slightly red in anger.

"Sit down, Sophia," he ordered. His voice dropped a few octaves as he glared at her. She hesitated slightly like she was fighting an invisible pull. "Now," he said a touch louder, his voice having even more bass and authority. Everyone was clearly shocked to hear that from him; especially with it geared towards Sophia.

"Why are you defending her?" Sophia pouted as she plopped back down in her seat dramatically.

"She's new, she's a retired beta's granddaughter, and you're purposely trying to embarrass her," Liam answered easily. Against myself, my heart dropped a little. He defended me, but for all the wrong reasons. I was expecting... I had no idea what I was expecting.

"Alpha, she doesn't know," Mya said lowly as she looked at her food. It was the same volume and quickness she talked to Kaden in earlier. The one that wasn't meant for my ears.

"Doesn't know what?" he asked low and quick, following Mya's lead.

"Anything. She has no idea what she is," Mya answered, her lips barely moving. What the hell were they talking about? Was I not a normal senior in high school just like them? Well, I knew now I obviously wasn't completely normal, but how different could I be? I couldn't take all the questions and secrets anymore. Against my better judgement, I took a deep breath and closed my eyes tightly before I grazed Mya's hand.

The black turned to film. It was everyone at the table, including me. They were standing naked in a bare spot in the woods. Suddenly, their bones started snapping as they all morphed; bringing them all to their knees. I kept the surprised scream I wanted to let out on the back of my throat. Fur sprouted, faces morphed and changed until there were wolves on all fours instead of naked people on two feet. Liam was the largest, he led the group; the Alpha. Sophia flaked him on his left side and Daniella... Daniella stayed hidden in the tree line. Only her silver eyes giving her away. The vision faded away to a black glassy haze, leaving a heavy throbbing pain in my head. I dropped my hand into my lap and waited for the haze to disappear completely before opening my eyes. Everyone had moved on with their conversations until I brought attention back to myself by shooting out of the chair and backing away from them.

"What the hell?" I breathed as I looked at the table full of werewolves.

6. One Touch

Liam was the first to stand as he approached me. With every step he took towards me, I took one away from him. He was trying to touch me, and I couldn't let that happen. He was a freak. They were all freaks...

I was a freak.

Liam wanted to comfort me and explain, but he was unsure of himself. He was frustrated at his unsureness. There was also want. He wanted me, but he was conflicted because he had Sophia. Eventually, it turned to knowing.

"You know, don't you? Just like you knew my name before I even told you," he asked, trying to keep the conversation between us.

"M-Mya told me," I lied. A hush fell over the cafeteria as they watched me back away from their leader. Apparently, disobeying him was frowned upon. Another thing I didn't understand. Liam noticed my dodgy eyes and looked back at the curious faces with a growl before he stepped directly to me, passing me in the process.

"Come with me," he muttered towards me on the way out. I stutter-stepped before I followed him out quickly. I didn't want to be alone with Liam by any means, but staying in the cafeteria with all the eyes on me was worse. Liam walked briskly, and I had to jog to keep up with him. He left the school building out the back and went into a tree line nearby. My head was still pounding as I breathed heavily trying to keep up with him. Physical activity wasn't my strong suit and gravity wasn't my friend, so I more stumbled after him than jogged. The cold wasn't helping either. Even after walking for a few minutes, he continued.

"Okay, s-stop!" I yelled at him, shivering. My coat and scarf were still in my locker and I was completely vulnerable to the ice winds. He stopped and whipped around to face me, catching me off guard. I ran right into him. The hairs on my arms reached for him, even in the cold. I could feel him all around me. He tried to catch me, but it only made me freak out even more as I tried to get away from him.

"D-don't t-touch me!" I said, falling onto my butt. He huffed out a breath before crossing his arms and watching me stand up on my own. He grabbed my clothed arm as he stood in front of me.

"What are you?" he asked firmly.

"What am I? What are you?!" I retorted in frustration as I pushed him away from me. He growled low in warning as his canines extended further down.

"Never, push me away," he warned. I was too stunned to argue back. Stunned and scared. I'd never seen anything like that in my life. Well, once.

"Just like Sophia," I breathed out before my brain could tell my mouth not to talk. That only made him angrier.

"Sophia growled at you?" he asked, getting even angrier. I sighed and shook my head as I crossed my arms over my chest in a lame attempt to get warm. I really hated the cold.

"Yes. No. Not really... kind of... I don't know how to explain it. I don't even know what it is. I don't know what's happening, but ever since I got to this weird backwards town, things have been... weird," I struggled to find the right words. He didn't look happy with my answer.

"Try," he ordered, I glared at him.

"Stop using that tone on me; it only pisses me off," I told him before I took a breath to calm down. I shook my arms out to try and get some heat into them before I crossed them back. "Look, I don't know what's happening to me. I've always been an empath. Picking up on people's emotions and intentions has always been easy. But ever since I got here, it's been... intense. I'm reading people's minds. When I touch someone, a scene plays out before me like a movie or video. My vision hazes, my eyes go weird, I get these pounding headaches," I admitted, just ranting for the sake of getting it out at this point. "The first person I touched today was Sophia. My scene of her portrayed her as... feral and vicious. Her teeth extended like yours just did and she was glaring and growling at me. The scene wasn't clear cut in the picture it showed but the meaning was clear to me. She was jealous of me, for reason's I don't get at all, and she wanted to destroy me at this school," I finished. I turned away from him and ran my fingers through my hair and tugged on it slightly as I tried to make sense of it. The more I tried, the less I understood. Nothing was coming together.

"What did you see when I touched you?" he asked, calmer now. I hesitated and began chewing on my cheek. It was a really bad habit of mine. I felt urged to tell him, but it was embarrassing. I couldn't look at him. I was compelled to tell him. I wanted to get it off of my chest and see, once and for all, if I was imagining it.

"We were laying in a forest. Y-You kissed me and told me that you loved me. Then you ripped my heart out of my chest and left with Sophia," I explained, looking at my feet. He was quiet for a long moment.

"What does that mean?" he asked hoarsely. He cleared his throat as I finally looked at him. He had pink creeping up his neck. I'd caught him off guard. I released a breath and looked at my feet.

"You lust for me... you may even feel some kind of connection to me like... we belong together or something, but you'll choose her," I explained timidly, my voice tapering off towards the end. He heard me anyway. I was too embarrassed to look at him. Embarrassed because I felt the same about him. Embarrassed because the vision actually hurt, and seeing them together at lunch only confirmed my suspicions. And I didn't have that claim on him. I didn't know him well enough to feel for him the way I did.

"That's why you told me to stay away from you," he noted as a partial question even though he already knew the answer. I shrugged. He took a step towards me and despite my shivering and my knowledge of his much warmer skin, I took a step back to keep my distance. When I looked up, my eyes were caught by his.

"It's a lot more complicated than that," he protested. I held a hand up to stop him.

"One, I just moved here and you don't even know me. You're not qualified to even have feelings for me yet. Plus, you're with Sophia, and I get that. Two, I may not know what's been happening with me lately, and they've never come like this, but my gut is always right when it comes to someone's emotions and intentions. It's never been wrong. It told me you were with Sophia before I even knew your name. I'm not stupid Liam. I know you love her, and I don't care. It's none of my business and it doesn't bother me at all," I said. The last part was a lie, but he didn't need to know that.

"How does it work?" he asked after a moment, changing the subject. I shrugged.

"Honestly, I have no idea. They didn't start happening like this until to-day," I admitted as I tried to warm my arms. We were both silent as we avoided eye contact. Liam didn't seem to even notice the cold.

"And you seriously have no idea what we are? What you are? I can smell the wolf in you. How have you not shifted yet?" he asked.

"Considering the fact that I don't even know that you're talking about, 'I don't know' seems like the appropriate answer," I said.

"Where have you been? This is basic stuff, born into your blood. This is taught to us practically as soon as birth. It's your life; you're livelihood," he rambled.

"My dad's an ambassador. We traveled a lot. I never stayed in one place for more than three years. I-I didn't even know my real mother's name until yesterday, so cut me some slack," I snapped at him. His defense softened.

"I'm sorry," he said softly and sincerely. I shook my head. It was all I could do. It was a different conversation for a different time. "How old are you... exactly," he asked.

"Almost 18, why?" I asked.

"Because you haven't shifted yet and that's typically something that should have happened already," he answered. "Maybe I could try to show you by touching you, or something?" he asked, holding his hand out towards me. I looked at it unsurely as I readjusted my arms. My breathing created a small cloud in front of me.

"I don't even know if that's how it works," I said. He only shrugged.

"Then it can't hurt to try, can it?" he countered. I didn't want to touch him. He'd already seen my eyes change before and knew everything so why was I hesitating?

I didn't want to feel hopelessly drawn to him like before...

I sighed before I gave in and took his hand in mine. I gasped as the picture changed rapidly this time. I was thrown into a warmer day in a different part of the forest. The sun was shining down, warming my skin with it's rays. The birds were quiet. There was Liam, too, but he was much younger. Maybe around 8 years old. He was with his father; a clone of him. Liam groaned in pain, his bones cracking slowly, one at a time. His body demanding him to morph into a beast. He was screaming, crying on his knees, grasping the dirt that couldn't save him.

"You're fine, son. It's the most natural thing in the world for us. Don't fight your wolf; it's only going to make it harder. Embrace it, son. It's a onetime pain," his father instructed him as he circled the poor boy. I watched as each bone broke until he was fully a wolf. I felt bad for the boy, but Liam viewed it as if it were the most natural thing in the world. He was relieved that it finally happened. He was proud.

"You're Alpha blood will eventually take over and you'll grow to be the largest. Well, second largest," the father joked, referring to himself. The small wolf wagged his tail as his head tilted slightly. He circled his father playfully before they tussled together. The father was proud and laughing.

The vision shifted, sending a jolt through my head. There was an image of the entire pack as wolves. I saw who stood next to his father as his best friend and Beta, I saw Liam's mother, the Luna, and Liam's sisters. I saw his life in fast forward. I learned what he learned, saw what he saw.

I couldn't help but to notice that Sophia was always there. He really loved her. I saw the memory of when she finally shifted and they realized they weren't mates. I saw them make a pact to pretend. They were happy together, after all. I saw his thoughts when he first saw me and what we were to each other. I saw what I was supposed to mean to him.

The stabbing, throbbing pain in my head got to be too much and I let go quickly. There were unwanted tears in my eyes as I waited for the haze to fade and Liam to come back into focus. I took a step away from him as I tried to swallow the lump in my throat. My head pounded painfully, but that wasn't what I was worried about at the moment.

"There's no way," I breathed. I took another step back as I held my forehead, trying to squeeze away the pain. I shut my eyes tightly and tried to wait for it to pass. With one touch, knowing about werewolves was second nature. It was like I was born into it instead of just finding out. The rank structure, the history, it just came easily to me. But one thing in particular terrified me.

"What did you see?" he asked hesitantly.

"Everything," I whispered, opening my eyes slowly. "We're nothing to each other. We can't be mates," I said unsurely.

"We are," he said softly.

"Everyone already thinks your mate is Sophia, so how can we mean anything to each other?" I asked as I moved my hand. I was getting dizzy but I needed answers. Liam looked at me with worry as he stepped closer.

"Are you okay?" he asked. I was confused until I felt the thick liquid from my nose, touch my lip. I touched it curiously, thinking my nose was just running from the numbing cold. I looked at my finger through my black-spotted vision to see the crimson red smear. It was blood. I muttered something incoherent as the world began to spin and I lost more of my sight. I tried to stay conscious but my body shut down on its own accord.

7. Alphas

My breathing labored as consciousness returned. It felt like I'd just finished running ten miles, and I wasn't athletic at all. It was a moment before my eyes adjusted to the moonlit room and I remembered what happened. The previous visions hit me all my once, causing my head to pound again. I groaned as I turned on my side, facing the open window. It was nighttime. My grandparents were probably freaking out right now. I didn't recognize the room, but it smelled like pine and mint leaves. It was Liam's smell. This must have been his room. I touched under my nose to find it dry now. No sign that it had even bled.

Throwing the covers off, I stood on unstable legs and made my way to the door. I felt so weak. My knees wobbled and shook as I braced myself against anything I could find. I opened the door to a hallway. I used the wall to support me as I went to the end of the hallway and found the stairs. I took it one step at a time and by the time I hit the bottom, I was panting again. I rested a hand on my knee and the other on the railing.

"Daniella?" Liam asked before I felt his hand on my back. Pine and mint leaves. His smell was intoxicating. His touch gave me goosebumps as a chill ran down my spine. I liked it way too much. I slowly moved away from him and turned to look at him.

"One, its Dani. And two, don't touch me," I said hoarsely.

"You can barely walk, let me help you," he practically begged. I didn't want him to touch me, but he was right. I swallowed my pride and eventually let him. I was careful not to touch his skin. My body reacted on its own and purred at his touch. I tried to ignore it. He took me to the living room where his two sisters were watching TV. Isabel was 16 years old and Lily was 6 years old.

Isabel had chocolate brown hair with natural highlights. Her eyes shined a gorgeous ocean blue. Her skin looked like sun-kissed porcelain. She was tall... taller than me for sure, and gorgeous. She preferred to be called Bella, I remembered from Liam's memories.

Lily's looks were more innocent with honey-colored curls and blue, doe-like eyes. Both of them looked like their mother with high cheekbones, full lips, and thick eyelashes. Isabel's eyebrows were perfectly manicured and arched. Even though I'd never met them in person before, I knew everything about them through Liam's mind.

I was tempted to greet them, but instead, I stayed quiet as Liam sat me on the couch next to Lily. They both looked at me curiously, trying to figure out who I was, and who I was to Liam. Lily's intentions were pure curiosity. She'd never seen a new face in town before. Bella was more protective. She wanted to know what I wanted with her brother and why I was here.

"Lily, Bella, this is Dani. She just moved here," Liam introduced me. I could sense the sentence he wanted to use hanging in the air.

She's my mate.

He didn't say it though. He kept it to himself. He didn't want anyone to know. He tried to prop me up on a pillow, but I stopped him with a simple glare. He sighed before giving Bella a warning look.

"I'm going to grab something from the kitchen... behave," he said before he left me to the piranhas. They had no intention of leaving me be. Bella was the first to turn her cautious glance at me.

"Who are you?" she spat rudely.

"The retired beta's granddaughter," I answered, knowing she was asking about my status and not the name she already knew.

"Why haven't I seen you before?" she followed on. I relaxed against the couch and rubbed my forehead to alleviate some of the leftover pain.

"My father and I left when I was an infant. I just came back yesterday. I don't know why," I answered, predicting her next question.

"What are you doing here?" Bella asked. I had nothing to hide, but I knew Liam didn't want anyone knowing what I was to him. I kept to the semi-truth.

"That would be a question for your brother. I didn't know anything about werewolves until today. He told me during school and I passed out. I really don't know what happened after that. Then I woke up here," I explained, keeping out the part where I saw Liam's whole life like it was a movie. I didn't even know how to really explain that. Bella had it on her mind to tell Sophia as soon as possible. Apparently, they were close. I was correct of course, as I watched her pull out her phone and start typing away.

"Do you know how to play house?" Lily asked, her innocence leaking through her words. I nodded with a smile and moved to the floor carefully to sit near her dollhouse that was set in the middle of the living room floor. She handed me a Barbie and I played along. Bella's hatred towards me lessened slightly at seeing me play with her little sister, but I really didn't care what she thought. It was a few minutes before Liam came back with water, aspirin, and crackers. He stopped just inside the living room and smiled gently at us. I could feel his adoration for the two of us and it was doing weird things to me.

"Stop that," I said to him. He looked at me confused. "Stop thinking what you're thinking," I clarified.

"Don't act like you know my brother. You don't even know what he's thinking," Bella said in her brother's defense.

"I'm really good at reading faces," I lied easily. Liam sat next to me and handed me the medicine and water. I took it before he offered me the crackers.

"This is just a little something to hold you over until dinner," he offered. I looked at him in confusion.

"You must be high. I'm not staying for dinner," I said defiantly at the same time Bella protested as well. Liam growled protectively at Bella in my defense. I could tell that the growl took him by surprise as he stopped and blinked at himself.

"What's high?" Lily asked in pure curiosity.

"Nothing," Liam dismissed his little sister. He turned his attention back to me as he tried to shake it off. "You're staying for dinner, and then you're spending the night. You can't even walk by yourself. You're staying close until you're better. I've already cleared it with your grandparents and Nora dropped off a bag for you while you were sleeping," he explained. I was furiously. I couldn't believe my grandparents were okay with this. It felt like a betrayal.

"You can't make me stay here!" I yelled as I stood quickly. The sudden movement made me sway as I blacked out for a moment. Liam's hands steadied me as he sat me back down on the couch.

"My point exactly. You're not well, and you're not leaving my sight until you feel better. No matter how long it takes," he said. I knew why he was doing this. It was mostly his wolf. He was worried about me. Regardless, he was pulled to take care of me.

"My father wants to see you," Liam said flatly as he scooped me into a cradle. I knew it would be pointless to protest being carried so I settled for huffing out a breath and crossing my arms.

"This is kidnapping, you know. You can't keep me here against my will," I pouted. He only sighed and held me close as he navigated through his house. I hated that I loved the way his touch made me feel. He knocked on a door before pushing it open and closing it with his foot behind us. He set me down carefully on my feet as I glared at him briefly.

"Daniella; it's nice to finally meet you," Liam's father, Alpha Connor greeted me, pulling my attention away from Liam. He stood in front of his desk and reached his hand out to shake mine. I looked at it hesitantly. I didn't want to be rude, but the last time was too much.

"Dad," Liam said protectively as he sat me in one of the chairs in front of the desk. Alpha Connor dropped his hand quickly.

"Right, the thing. Sorry, I forgot," he replied before he sat in the edge of his desk. So Liam already told him about me and my "thing"... great. Alpha Connor stared at me, or more specifically, my eyes. He looked like an older version of Liam with his good looks. Liam growled lowly at his father after he had been staring too long for his liking. Alpha Connor chuckled lightheartedly.

"Protective, are we?" the Alpha said to his son. I stared at Liam out of the corner of my eye, daring him to say something.

"She doesn't feel well," he said. That was all he said. I kept my eyes on Alpha Connor. I couldn't look at Liam anymore. It just made me want to strangle him.

8. You're My Secret

A lpha Connor watched the two of us curiously. He was intrigued by our dynamic. He was reminded of when he and his wife first met. Well, a more anger-charged version of it.

He knew.

At least he thought he did. I averted my eyes to the ground to hide the hints of pain and shame that were apparent on my face. Just like before, just like my first vision of Liam, he stayed quiet. I was his secret. I would be secret. I regained my composure before I looked at Alpha Connor.

"I'd like to go home now," I said.

"You're staying," Liam growled. I felt angry tears of frustration blur my vision but I tried to hold them back.

"Oh really? Why?" I challenged him. The air was charged with tension as Liam just glared in the silence.

"Stay for dinner at least. I wouldn't be comfortable sending you home hungry. I'll make sure you get home afterwards. You have my word," the Alpha offered. I knew that that was the best I was going to get for now. I stood carefully with a quiet thank you before I slowly made my way out of the room. I didn't know where I was going, but I had to be away from that tense atmosphere. It rattled my nerves. I felt him before I saw him. Liam caught up to me in the hallway but he, thankfully, didn't touch me.

"Why are you being so difficult?" he asked in frustration as he stood in front of me.

"Why are you denying me?" I countered as a stubborn tear finally fell. I didn't want him to see me cry, but they were tears of frustration. I wished that I'd never touched him in the woods. I would have continued on blissfully naïve and unaware. Knowing what I was to him and what it meant made it harder. It made it hurt more.

He didn't answer me as he released a breath and looked away from me. He didn't say it, but I felt his answer. It was because he loved her. He wanted to be with her. He always had been. Even with his mate standing right in front of him.

"I thought so," I said softly. As another tear trailed down my cheek. "I'm tired," I said softly. He moved to pick me up but I put a hand up to stop him. He sighed before he just turned and led the way slowly, looking back at me every once in a while. He led me back to his room and I got in the bed and pulled the covers around me as he just watched me. I felt like protecting myself from his stare by throwing the blanket over my face, but that felt childish so I turned over to give him my back instead.

"Dani, I'm sorry, really. I just want to make sure you're okay," he apologized.

"That's not what this is about and you know it," I said bitterly. "Just, leave me alone... please," I asked. He hesitated before he eventually sighed and moved to somewhere else in the room. He set a pair of sweatpants and a shirt on a chair in the room.

"In case you want to shower," he said. He gave me another look before he left, closing the door behind him. I sat up and stared at the clothes. It looked like he'd had the sweats for a while. They didn't look like they could fit him now, but they looked loved.

A shower actually sounded wonderful. I gingerly took the clothes to the bathroom and set them on the counter of the sink as I stared the water in the standing shower. I looked through different drawers before I finally found a towel. I still felt weak but a shower was too tempting to deny. I stripped my clothes from my body and tested the water before getting in. The hot water that pelted my body was relaxing. I let out a breath in content as I let my eyes close. I let the water run over the top of my head and soak my hair so the water touched every inch of my body. The steam only intensified the pine and mint smell mixed with the smell of fresh rain and mangos. The combination was calming. I knew it had a lot to do with Liam's scent, but I accepted it in my solitude anyway.

By the time I got out of the shower, I felt a lot better. I could walk a little easier and I didn't feel as weak. I dried myself off before drying my hair as well. When I went back to the bedroom, a backpack sat on my bed. I looked inside to see my toiletries. I sighed and found my brush before running it through my hair. It was calming and therapeutic, and I ended up doing it longer than necessary.

The door swung open and I expected Liam to come back with his tail between his legs, but it wasn't him. Compared to the alternative, I wished it was him. I could easily sense her fury and jealousy. She didn't just show up to 'talk'. She intended to intimidate and harm me. Bella must have gotten very creative in that text, definitely leaving out the part that I didn't even want to be here.

"What the hell are you doing here?" she asked heatedly.

"Liam is forcing me to stay, or did Bella forget to mention that part?" I sad indifferently, knowing that it wouldn't make a difference to her. I was too tired for her crap. She shook her head.

"You're lying," she insisted. "Why would he want you here? Why are you wearing his clothes?" she asked.

"I took a shower," I said, only answering the last question.

"Take it off," she growled.

"I'd rather not be completely naked," I countered.

"Where is Liam?" she yelled at me.

"Hell if I know," I shrugged. If she wanted to be mad over something that wasn't even my fault that was on her. She should have been talking to the one forcing me to be here in the first place. But of course, she would never blame him.

9. Luna

"Are you looking for Liam, Sophia?" Luna Addie asked as she stood in the doorway of the bedroom. Sophia and I both whipped around to look at her; neither of us heard her entrance. The quick motion unsteadied me slightly.

Luna Addie's full name was Adelaide, but she preferred Addie. She was a vision of beauty, pose, grace, and perfection. She was always a great mother to her kids and she cared greatly for her pack. Her wavy brown hair was pulled away from her face and into a ponytail. Her cheekbones sat high near her almond-shaped hazel eyes. Her figure was to die for. She was tall with curves in all the right places. Her athletic build was accentuated by her compression tank top and black spandex capris. She looked like she just finished working out.

She knew the real reason Sophia was here. She seemed to know that Sophia saw me as a personal threat, but felt the need to protect me, almost mother-ly. Luna Addie played unaware on purpose. Sophia bowed her head slightly in embarrassment for being caught by the Luna with her green monster showing.

"Y-Yes, I am, Luna. Have you seen him?" Sophia answered terribly. It was clearly a lie. She already found what she was looking for.

"He went for a run. You can probably find him out back. But please make your visit quick, we're having company for dinner tonight," Luna Addie answered diplomatically. Sophia thanked her quietly before giving me a look that told me to back off; he would always be hers.

As if I didn't already know that. I released a breath as my eyes stung again with unshed tears against my will. I didn't want to feel so strongly towards Liam, but I hated Sophia for being in the way. It had only been a day and I was already tired of my babyish reaction to a fact I knew from the start. I hated knowing. I attempted to dry my face discreetly as I faced Luna Addie again.

"I'm Luna Addie. You must be Dani," she introduced herself to me. I nodded, not trusting my voice at the moment. "It can't be easy for you," she said as she came closer. I held in the sniffle that wanted to be let out to kick start my tears. I wouldn't let it happen.

"I don't know what you're talking about," I lied. I knew exactly what she meant. Somehow, she picked up on the fact that Liam and I were mates, and it only took her all of two minutes.

"He's an idiot... my son. Ignoring a great catch that was literally made for him for something so... bland, but familiar," she continued. I felt the stubborn tear fall despite my efforts. I knew she was trying to console and comfort me, but the wounds were too fresh and it stung anyway. I had nothing to add. I was embarrassed that my eyes were probably red and puffy over Liam.

"Your mother was my best friend. I miss her a lot. We grew up together, you know? Liam told me that you haven't shifted yet, and you didn't even know about... well, any of what we are until today at school," she said, changing the subject off of her son. I nodded.

"It was... taxing, but now I feel as if I've known my whole life," I explained.

"Yes, your gift of sight and moon-kissed eyes. You were actually born during a full moon, you know? I was actually there. You almost didn't make it. Your heart stopped while you were still in the womb, but your mother refused to let you die. They wanted to send her in for an emergency c-section, but they feared they were already too late, so Beck used her own claws to rip her stomach open to get you out. The bleeding was too much though, and there were only enough available hands to work on one of you. You still weren't breathing, and your mother wouldn't let them touch her until you were awake and crying, but by the time that happened, it was too late for your mother," Luna Addie explained, throwing herself back in time.

She was deep in thought. I wanted to see what happened. I wanted to see my mother, but I knew I was too weak to try it. It would have to be another time when I was sure I was strong enough for whatever it was. She sighed and touched my back gently. I flinched out of habit from the scars I received there from Evelyn. Luna Addie either didn't notice or didn't acknowledge it as she let her hand fall to her side.

"Dinner will be ready in half an hour," she said before she left the room, closing the door behind her. I sat on the bed before enveloping myself in Liam's blanket and laying down. I wanted to cry and smile at the same time. His smell was comforting, but it wasn't mine to take comfort in. I sighed and closed my eyes. Maybe if I just slept here, I wouldn't have to sit through what was sure to be the most awkward dinner of my life. I could already see me having to explain my lie as to why I don't eat meat to Liam's entire family.

I relaxed and drifted off into a light sleep. Suddenly I was in the forest. Liam's wolf trotted to the end of the tree line just as Sophia turned to continue her pacing in a field. She was wearing the same clothes as the ones she came to see me in. The vision was of today. It could've been right this moment even. She was furious, but her face just held a pout. Liam shifted back and threw his basketball shorts on.

"What are you doing here?" he asked. It took Sophia by surprise. Hell, it even took Liam by surprise. Sophia had dropped in whenever she wanted all the time and he'd always welcomed her, but not so much this time.

"Bella wanted me to come over," she lied. Liam rolled his eyes with a sigh.

"Of course she did," he muttered.

"Your mom told me to leave. And that new girl is stalking you or some-thing. I caught her in your room. And she was even wearing your clothes," Sophia said as she crossed her arms. Liam was just happy to hear that I accepted his clothes. Sophia didn't like the satisfied look on his face at all.

"Sophia, don't play dumb. I know that you know exactly who she is to me," Liam warned her.

"I'm your mate, as far as anyone else is concerned," she whined. He glared slightly in annoyance.

"I know, and that's the way it'll stay for now, but you have to leave Dani alone. I mean it. No petty games or trying to embarrass her. The more you do, the more my wolf wants to get rid of you... permanently. I'll still protect her above you, its instinct. Don't forget that," he explained. They took a breath and calmed down a bit.

"So what do we do now?" she asked.

"Nothing," he said as he pulled a nearby shirt over his head. "No one knows who she is, and we'll keep it that way," he answered. Sophia was satisfied with his answer and hoped his attitude towards the situation stuck. She wanted nothing more than to be the next Luna.

"Your mom knows," Sophia countered. "When I left, your mom was consoling her. She said it couldn't be easy for her." I didn't even know she heard that much.

"She could've been talking about anything, Sophia. I'm not about to jump to conclusions," Liam said as he began walking back towards the house slowly while holding Sophia's hand.

"She knows, Liam. And if you want to keep us a thing, you need to stop being so nice to that girl. The more you ignore her, the easier it'll be," Sophia advised. He leaned over and captured her lips with his in a kiss. My heart ached at the sight.

"I just had to make sure she was okay. I couldn't just leave her on the ground in the cold," he countered. She stood in front of him and trailed a finger down the front of his shirt seductively as she bit her lip through her smirk.

"Well, if you want, after she leaves tonight, I'll let you take care of me all you want. And I can take care of you, too," she said seductively. The thought of sex with Liam was heavy on her mind from experience. My heart squeezed tighter at that. I don't know why I expected him to be a virgin, but for some reason, I did. It made me want to stay the night just to spite her. He would feel too guilty to do anything with his mate in the house, and I knew it. Liam kissed her goodbye with the promise to text her later before he went into the house and straight to his room.

The room was dim as the sun dropped to sleep for the day. He looked at my sleeping figure in conflict. He cared for the curled up innocent girl on his bed, but he didn't know what to do about it. He loved Sophia; he was in love with Sophia, but I was his literal soul mate. The problem was, I was too new, too different, and too unfamiliar. I scared him a bit. He didn't know me, and I didn't know him.

I was a werewolf who, at 17 years old, hadn't shifted yet. I was a wolf who didn't even know what she was until a few hours ago. I was the wolf with the moon-kissed eyes and an unexplainable gift of sight. I was the wolf with the mysterious past. I was the wolf who was his mate.

He leaned over and kissed my forehead as he pushed a strand of hair away from my face. I looked troubled, even in my sleep. My eyes were still puffy, and my face was red and blotchy from crying. He felt bad and guilty. He knew he was the cause of my tears, but it still wasn't enough to make him change his mind.

10. I'm Not Her

I woke with my headache gone. Someone was shaking me gently. My eyes opened in the dim room and adjusted to see Liam. He was sitting on the edge of the bed near me. My eyes spilled over with tears from the dream that I knew was reality. I sniffled as my body shook with silent sobs. I was too tired to have my guard up. Liam was instantly worried.

"Hey, it's okay. It was just a bad dream," he tried to console me. It only made me angrier because I knew it wasn't a dream. I shook my head.

"It wasn't a dream," I cried.

"What happened?" he asked as his hand moved to my shoulder to comfort me. I jerked away from him angrily. It was insulting that he was going to try to ignore me and comfort me at the same time.

"We know who she is, but no one else needs to know. Do nothing; just ignore her," I said quoting him. "And your mom does know, by the way. She called you an idiot, and rightfully so," I said, calming my tears slightly. He looked at me shocked.

"You saw all of that? Were you there? Did you follow me?" he questioned. I threw the covers off of me and stood carefully.

"I didn't follow you. I was sleeping. I guess I dreamt it," I tried to explain.

"How much of it did you see?" he had the audacity to ask. I narrowed my eyes at him as I crossed my arms.

"You know what, just take me home so Sophia can properly 'take care' of you... again," I ordered angrily.

"Dinner is literally in five minutes," he argued.

"Your plan to ignore me only works if I'm not around. Follow the plan, remember?" I snapped at him. I couldn't help it, I was hurt. I wanted to claw Sophia's eyes out, and I didn't even have claws yet.

"You promised you would stay for dinner," he said stubbornly.

"Yeah, well I don't make it a habit to stay where I'm not wanted," I countered. I sighed and ran a hand down my face. "Forget it, I'll walk home if I have to," I said, more muttering to myself as I went to gather my things. Liam's hand touched my back. I flinched away from him so fast, you would've thought his hand was on fire.

"Don't touch me!" I yelled at him as I spun to face him. There was fear written in my face. Liam took a beat before he took a step back.

"What happened to you?" he asked softly. I hated that he saw right through my fear. I didn't want to answer that question. Saying that 'my evil step-mother tortured me' was just too cliché and I didn't want his pity. He didn't deserve to know anyway. He didn't deserve to know anything about me.

"What's all the yelling about?" Luna Addie asked as she entered the room. She was now dressed in a peach blouse and a pair of black slacks; untouched by the cold. Her expression softened when she saw my face. "What did you do, Liam?" she asked accusingly.

"Why do you assume it's me?" he asked with a hint of a whine. She only gave him a knowing look as her arms crossed over her chest.

"Well, for one, you're not the one who's hurt, but you are an idiot," she said. Had I not been so devastated, I might have laughed.

"You really do know, don't you? Sophia said you did," Liam muttered to himself. Hearing him say her name made me flinch as I cast my eyes down to look at my feet. Luna Addie growled at Liam.

"She should have backed off the second she knew. You should have broken ties with her the second you knew," Luna Addie said disapprovingly.

"You liked her," Liam said confused.

"Because I thought she was a respectable girl. But if she was, she would've gotten out of the way the second you told her you found your mate. Both of you should be ashamed of yourselves," she chastised her son.

"Mom," Liam began.

"Don't start," she stopped him sternly as her eyes shot to him. "I'm very disappointed in you, Liam. I thought I raised you better than that. You will not force this girl to do anything; especially when you won't even claim her as your mate. If she wants to leave, you can't make her stay. You don't have that right," she said diplomatically. It felt good to have someone stick up for me, but I couldn't help wishing that it would've come from Liam.

"I want to go home," I said to Luna Addie. I turned to Liam, but I couldn't look him in the eyes. I didn't want to get stuck in them again. "And I want you to leave me alone. Out of sight, out of mind, right?" I said flatly.

"I'll take you home," Luna Addie offered. I thanked her quietly before grabbing the bag and heading towards the door.

"Dani," Liam pleaded. I hesitated before I continued out and into the hallway with Luna Addie right beside me. She helped me down the stairs and led the way to their garage where four different cars sat. She chose an Escalade and unlocked the doors remotely. I got in and slammed the door behind me as the garage door went up. I was angry and upset, but I didn't want to seem rude to Luna Addie who was only trying to help.

"Sorry," I apologized for the door as I looked to her. She shook her head as she backed out of the driveway. The heat began blasting through the air vents.

"I'm the one who should be apologizing. My son is an idiot. I thought I taught him better than this," she said through clenched teeth. "My advice? When he finally comes to his senses, make him work for it," she said, gritting her teeth even more. I think she was even more pissed off than I was. I readjusted in the seat as I watched the passing scenery from the window. The rest of the ride was quiet but I could feel her apologies and sympathy hang in the air. Finally, we made it to the Wilders' residents; my new home. I was hesitant to push the car door open, knowing I didn't have a jacket, and the cold only seemed to get worse when the sun set. I could feel the cold from the window.

"If you ever need anything, please don't hesitate to call me," Luna Addie said as she handed me a slip of paper with her number on it. I gave her a gentle smile.

"Thank you," I said sincerely as I took it. I had a feeling I would be needing it. I put my hand in the door handle and prepared myself for the cold as I grabbed my bag from the floor of the passenger seat.

"And if you don't feel like going ot school tomorrow, no one would blame you. Give yourself time, if you need it. I'll talk to Liam, but there's only so much I can do," she said guiltily.

"You don't have to do that. I want it to be his choice, not his burden," I said before I pushed the door open and quickly made my way inside the house. As soon as the front door opened, my grandparents were on me like crazy on a vegan. They wanted to know what happened, and how the Miller's house was. I only flinched when they mentioned Liam. I was tired and I just wanted to sleep for a while.

"Luna Addie brought me," I answered one of their questions. They looked confused.

"You know about...?" my grandma trailed off. I nodded.

"I don't know what's happening to me, but when I touch people, I see things...their intentions, their thoughts, their past... I touched Liam, and he showed me everything, but it made me pass out so he took me to his house and wouldn't let me leave. Luna Addie finally bailed me out," I answered vaguely. Although they probably already knew that seeing as they sent over my toiletries, but that was all I was willing to give.

"Liam, the Alpha's son? What did he want with you?" my grandpa asked innocently. I felt the tears threaten to kick up again but I held them back as I took a breath and clenched my jaw. After a moment, I was finally able to speak again.

"Nothing... he wanted nothing with me," I said softly, my voice betraying me at the end. By the looks on their faces and the feeling of pity I was getting from them, they knew.

"He's your mate," my grandma said out loud knowingly. There was no sense in denying it. I nodded once slowly as I tried to swallow the lump in my throat.

"I just want to go to bed," I said as I pushed the bag further up my shoulder and headed for the stairs.

"Have you had dinner yet? We made a vegetarian-friendly pasta," Grandma Nora offered. I couldn't even think about food with the way my stomach was churning.

"Thank you, but I'm not that hungry," I muttered before I disappeared up the stairs. I took a quick shower before burying myself in my mother's blanket. The smell was calming, but I still felt the hollow ache in my chest. I'd never stayed in one place long enough for a relationship, but this is what I imagined a really bad break up felt like. One thing I knew for sure though: there was no way in hell I was going to school tomorrow.

11. Arianrhod

My grandparents must have known I wasn't leaving my bed because I wasn't bothered at all the next morning. I wasn't completely devastated about Liam, but I sure as hell didn't want to face him, or them together. I woke on my own accord at 10 a.m. I felt sluggish and sick. I didn't have the motivation to move, so I didn't. I only got up to use the bathroom occasionally. I was too embarrassed to face even my grandparents. I was left alone, but I could sense when one of my grandparents would stand outside the door, tempted to check on me, only to change their mind at the last moment. They were trying to respect that I wanted to be left alone, but they were still worried about me.

I, being too embarrassed to leave my room, decided to use the time to try and Google about my newfound abilities on my laptop. The empath stuff came up no problem, but the rest of it was a bit hard to make sense of. Of course, searching about the visions just pulled up a bunch of ads for psychics. I tried searching for things related to the moon, moon goddess and werewolves. I just ended up with a lot of stories and folklore.

I was so engrossed in my research that I didn't leave the house for the next week as I tried to make sense of what was happening to me. If I were honest with myself, I was scared to be around people when I didn't know what the consequences would be. Plus, it was a good way to get my mind off of Liam, and it only worked half of the time. He wasn't consuming my every thought, but he did come to mind every now and then.

The most interesting thing I found during my research was about the Moon Goddess. There were stories of the Moon Goddess having the power to grant love and punish the evil. Another story said the Moon Goddess was directly connected with the Fates and could see the future to protect her creatures, the wolves. The depiction from werewolf knowledge is a glowing figure with flowing white hair, glowing skin, and blue orbs for eyes with irises that mirrored the moon like mine did. It had her in flowing gray Grecian-style clothing that seemed to flow around her without the need for wind.

My research for moon-like eyes got a completely different result. There was a lot of speculation about what it meant, and plenty of forums to prove it. I sighed heavily as I leaned back and took a break. It seemed like it was just something I would have to discover on my own. After the first week of research, I moved on to trying to control whatever was happening to me. I started by focusing on my grandparents thoughts whenever I saw them or felt them outside my door. The more I practiced, the clearer their thoughts were. It wasn't just a feeling anymore; it was as if the words of their thoughts were scrolling across the bottom of a TV screen. It wasn't so loud that it was all I could think about. I worked on turning it on and off, although that was proving to be a lot harder.

"I was wondering when you would stop running from your gift," a voice said from inside my room. I knew that voice.

I despised that voice.

I turned slowly, praying it was just a trick of the mind, but lo and behold, there she was, perched on my vanity with her legs crossed. I couldn't help the way my heart sped up in fear as adrenaline ran through my veins.

"You're not real. You died, and I'm just going crazy. This is another weird tick, that's all," I said, trying to convince myself and make her disappear. I backed myself into a corner and slid my back down the wall until I was curled up with my knees in my chest. She rolled her eyes and hopped down from her perch.

"I am real. You're not imagining me. I know you can feel that much," she said as she came closer. She was right. I felt a pull of connection to her, even though my brain was telling me to fear her from history and habit. She smiled as she motioned to herself.

"Surprise! I'm not really dead," she said sarcastically. I wanted to cry and scream for help, but habit told me to keep my mouth shut out of self-preservation. I didn't want to make it worse.

"How?" I asked in a whisper as I tried to hold my tears back. She sighed and sat on the edge of my bed.

"Well, for one, I can't actually die because I'm immortal. But if you want the actual steps of how I did it, I staged the accident, used a little magic to look dead, and then waited until you got older," she explained.

"Magic?" I asked. She sighed and rolled her eyes.

"I had to keep you in the dark when it came to your abilities. You were too young. Your father was the one who wanted to keep your wolf heritage a secret. Although, he should've just told you. Why do you think I stuck around?" she asked. I shrugged.

"You got a kick out of torture?" I guessed. Her eyes went fiery... literally. Her irises turned to flames for a quick second before she calmed down a hair.

"I did not 'get a kick' out of torturing a child, but it was the only way. The whip I used suppressed your abilities. It was enhanced that way a long time ago by a very old and very powerful goddess. You were a child, I had to at least pretend there was a reason for it. And when your powers did surface, I had to make you forget; which is where the force-fed chicken came in," she explained.

Evelyn was alive and standing right in front of me... my brain was still trying to process that.

"Why did it involve torture?" I asked, too scared to relax. "And why leave when I was 12 is that was the case?" I added.

"I left because it was time for you to begin learning, but he never told you," she explained. "As for the torture, the magic was not set up by me. Witches created their tools to restrict abilities and memories from enemies, not children. I couldn't control the form it came in," she answered.

"So you want me to believe that you beat me to protect me... from myself?" I asked confused. She nodded. I tried to read her to see if she was telling the truth, but I was getting nothing from her except a strange sense that we were connected. It felt like I was trying to read myself. I couldn't find her thoughts no matter how hard I concentrated. She rolled her eyes at me.

"You won't be able to read me, child. I'm not a mortal. My real name is Arianrhod. I am the goddess of the stars and the sky of Welsh origin. Goddess of beauty, the moon, and magic. More commonly referred to as the Moon Goddess by my children. But I prefer Aria," she explained. I stared at her not quite sure how to feel or what to do. I didn't believe it. That would mean that my childhood nightmare was the Moon Goddess herself. It was impossible.

"You can't be... there's no way," I said, trying to come to terms with what was happening, if it was even real. She wasn't the glowing white figure depicted from Liam's memories. This was Evelyn, not the Moon Goddess. She sighed heavily before she stood and changed into the exact depiction I was thinking of. My eyes bulged. Had I not already been sitting, I would've fallen over. She wasn't kidding.

"This," she said motioning to her body as it lit up the room. I had to squint with how bright she seemed to glow, "is just for flash. People fear you more when you look nothing like them. But I prefer my true Welsh image," she said, changing back into the red-headed figure I was more familiar with.

"I'm dreaming. I have got to be dreaming," I said to myself as I looked away from her.

"I would slap you to prove otherwise but you would only freak out more. You have seriously got to toughen up. I thought I would've helped you in some way by showing you the world can be a lot crueler than you know, but you're even more timid if that's even possible. Pull up your big girl panties and respect your gift. You're the only one who has anything like it," she said.

"I-I have no idea what I'm doing! I don't even know what I can do, or if I can turn it off, or if I'll pass out every time I use it even if it's an accident," I rambled.

"That was because of the New Moon. That's why I'm here. Watching you suffer was getting pathetic. You haven't left this house in two weeks, and for no other reason other than the fact that you're embarrassed. I even made the full moon closer to help you feel more energized and you didn't even notice! Do you know how often I pull the moon closer? Not often," she complained. She reminded me of an upset teenager. A giggle escaped my lips and I felt a little better.

"So you're going to teach me?" I asked unsurely. I was worried that 'teaching' involved more whips and undercooked chicken.

"No, not in the way you think. Like actual classes, no pain, just strain because you've never done it before. You are my Earthly representation after all, and you're embarrassing. Hiding from your mate and always feeling sorry for yourself. Grow a pair. Liam will come around, he's just being childish right now. And Sophia will get hers, too. There's an order of things in this world. She's going against it," the Moon Goddess/Evelyn/Arianrhod/Aria said. I had no idea what to call her. She wore too many hats. I was offended and relieved at the same time.

"What do I call you?" I asked confused. She laughed something that sounded like clear crisp bells.

"Aria will do. Evelyn seems a bit evil, doesn't she?" she asked as her head tilted slightly. Her perfect red curls falling over her shoulder slightly. I nodded slowly. She chuckled as she stood in front of me and offered me a hand up. I hesitated before I took it and stood in front of her. Her hands brushed my hair behind my shoulders before she placed a kiss on my forehead. I instantly felt ten times better. My anxiety was gone, and I felt... confident and happy.

"You're going to be just fine," she promised.

"What was that?" I asked curiously.

"A temporary mute on your visions until I can teach you how to block them out yourself. Tomorrow, you will go to school, and you can touch people without your eyes going all lunar. We'll start training tomorrow when you get back. It's a gift, not a burden," she explained before she disappeared.

I felt... better.

12. A Bit of Vengeance

The next morning, I didn't hate the thought of going to school. My grandparents looked shocked when I came down the stairs. I was already fully dressed and eating. Not that I wasn't eating before, but I was downstairs and out of my room. They watched me silently as I smeared butter on my toast and sat at the bar.

"Hi," my grandpa finally said unsurely. I chuckled when I noticed their faces.

"I feel better; you can stop looking at me like that. Oh, can I catch a ride to school?" I asked. Grandma Nora nodded, still quiet.

"Are you sure?" she asked. I nodded with a small smile on my lips.

"I can't hide in my room forever," I shrugged. They both nodded slowly. After a very quick breakfast, I grabbed my school bag and met my grandma at the truck. She glanced at me out of the corner of her eye the whole ride until we eventually parked in front of the school.

"You can always call me if you want to come home early. I'd understand," she said. I kissed her cheek.

"Thanks grandma," I said before I grabbed my bag and stepped into the freezing cold. I made it inside quickly and was instantly greeted with stares. It was like the first day all over again. But surprisingly, this time, it didn't even phase me. I went to my locker and found it stuffed with school books for my subjects.

"I asked for your schedule and got the books you needed in case you came back," Mya explained from beside me. I smiled as I turned my attention to her.

"Thanks, Mya. I really appreciate that," I said genuinely. She looked at me cautiously, like I would fall apart at any moment. I chuckled. "I'm fine Mya, seriously," I assured her. I felt like I was about to be reassuring people all day. You would think someone died.

"If you're sure," she said, not at all convinced. It felt good, not to feel completely embarrassed or sad, even if it is only temporary. I wished Aria had come earlier with this stuff. Although I still wasn't sure how I felt about that whole ordeal either. Mya said a quick goodbye before heading to her class. I started making my way to mine. I made it just before the bell, taking the same seat I had the first day, all the way in the back. I almost forgot Liam had this class too, until he walked in after the bell. His eyes immediately found mine. I stared back at him, not backing down this time, and not feeling completely infatuated either. He sat next to me and turned his full attention to me.

"Dani, I-" he started in a hushed voice. He looked guilty and apologetic.

"If an apology is about to come out of your mouth, don't waste your breath. I can already hear the lingering 'but I love her', making your apology empty," I hissed at him. He shut his mouth instantly and faced forward.

"That's what I thought," I muttered before paying attention to my classes. The rest of my classes were pretty mundane until lunch. Like before, I walked through with Mya, having a lunch of meat-free spaghetti today. I sat at the same table as last time, knowing they would come eventually. When they did, Sophia was trying to pretend that nothing was wrong, but everyone else at the table looked at me curiously as if I would spontaneously combust at any moment.

"Are you okay? What happened?" Caden asked genuinely. My eyes caught Liam's as I stared straight at him.

"I was sick to my stomach," I said, knowing Liam would pick up on the double meaning before giving Caden a reassuring smile. "Must have been the flu or something," I shrugged it off.

"Caden, I think you have a little something," Sophia said as she reached across the table and brushed imaginary dust off of his hand as an excuse to graze mine. I glared at her as I stood and leaned across the table at the same time a small growl came from Liam's lips.

"Here," I said, grasping her wrist in my hand. She looked at a loss for words, and Liam was simply shocked. Last time I touched someone, I passed out. I glared straight at Sophia as I pulled her slightly closer.

"This is what you were trying to do, right? I told you already, there was nothing weird going on with my eyes. And I get that you're threatened by me because you don't have the security of actually being Liam's true mate, but trust me, I don't want him either, honey," I said before dropping her hand and sitting back down in my seat. Everyone at the table was quiet as their eyes bulged. As far as they all knew, Sophia was Liam's true mate.

"O-of course they're mates," Caden said unsurely. I shrugged as I started examining my nail beds.

"They're not, actually. I met Liam's mate... poor girl. They both know who she is and where she is. But Liam here is too embarrassed to tell everyone the truth. He'd rather live in his lie," I explained. "She's okay though. If he was too much of a coward to acknowledge her, she's better off without him anyway," I said, looking straight at Liam as I said so.

"That girl could be lying," Sophia challenged. I smirked at her.

"The Moon Goddess doesn't lie though. And when the information is coming straight from her... well, I believe her. It's not wise to question a goddess, after all," I answered confidently. A murmur went around the table but Liam's eyes stayed on me. I could feel the fire and joy behind my eyes at Liam's expense, but I didn't care. I met his stare head on and refused to back down.

"Can I talk to you for a moment... in private," he more ordered than asked. I could feel the bass and authority in his voice but it had no effect on me.

"No... but you can go fuck yourself, or Sophia, your fake mate if that's what you prefer," I answered Red crawled up his neck in anger and embarrassment as he growled at me in warning.

"You will not speak to me like that," he ordered. I chuckled.

"Oh really? What are you going to do about it? I will speak to you however I damn well please. You can't hurt me. You can't lock me away. You can't keep me hostage. And even if you tried, I would be gone in seconds. You have no idea what I'm capable of," I challenged him, feeling more powerful with every word. Now the whole cafeteria was shocked at the way I was speaking to Liam.

"What are you doing, Dani?" he asked lowly. I quirked an eyebrow at him as I smirked back without answering. He would find out in due time. He wanted to play games, we could play games. The bell rang and I calmly packed away my empty container before leaving the lunchroom with Mya on my heels. Everyone's eyes were on us as we made our way to our lockers. I was the new town crazy person, but I didn't really care at the moment.

"Listen, I know you're new and all but no one talks to Liam Miller like that. He's-"

"The future Alpha... I know, and frankly, I don't care," I finished for her. "I've learned a lot in the last few weeks, and I don't care. I'm stronger than him, and his mom is on my side anyway," I said.

"You've met Luna Addie?" she deadpanned. I chuckled and nodded.

"Like I said: a lot has happened in the last few weeks," I said as I opened my locker and grabbed my books.

"Still, Sophia-"

"Is going to do what? Spread petty rumors about me? Bare her teeth? She's a brat who thinks she can have whatever she wants... even if it's not hers," I said, glaring slightly into the space.

"What happened to you?" Mya asked. I shrugged as I shut my locker.

"I grew a pair," I said before walking off to my next class.

More like I was given a pair of magical ones.

13. The Lunar Effect

By the time I got home, thanks to a ride from Mya, half of the confidence had worn off, I was still riding the high of the day's events. I knew that exposing Sophia wouldn't force Liam to acknowledge me, but whoever said you shouldn't take an eye for an eye, forgot to mention how great it felt. My grandparents weren't home yet. They were out doing errands or something based on the note they left me on the kitchen counter. I sighed and shrugged my jacket off before going to find something to snack on.

"Looks like your return went well," Aria said as she appeared out of nowhere, sitting on the kitchen stool. It made me jump and I damn near dropped the bowl I was holding. I found some leftover vegetable soup to warm up and popped it in the microwave.

"You could say that," I said as I finally turned to face her as I leaned against the counter. I couldn't help the wide smile on my face.

"What did you do to me yesterday?" I asked. She smirked.

"I told you, it was just a bit of a confidence boost. We're connected, Daniella," she said.

"You never really elaborated the how," I noted. She sighed and rested her chin on the palm of her hand as I pulled my soup from the microwave carefully.

"You're like... my Earthly being. You are your own person and all, and you live like every other wolf, but there are perks. You have a direct line to my powers... all of them; seeing the future, sensing danger future and current, strength with your wolf, seeing people's true intentions and memories, healing people and things, blah, blah, blah, and you're nearly invisible. You can still be killed, but it's more difficult. You have a direct line to me. If you call me, I'll hear you first and come if you really need it. I'm an extra power source for you, which you might need during a full moon because that's when you're most vulnerable. Try not to do too much during new moons. It'll drain the shit out of you. It's when you're the weakest. It's the whole reason you passed out last time. Great timing with that, by the way," she said sarcastically as I grabbed a spoon and began eating as I listened.

"Why does a new moon weaken me?" I asked, before testing the next spoonful I had raised to my lips.

"Well, the moon is your main source of energy. I'm not actually a human or wolf so I'm not bound by the Earth. I get the moon's full powers all the time, but you have to be more careful. A new moon has the power to make you as weak as any other wolf for that day, and only a day. You have other sources to pull energy from, but you have to make more of an effort to do so. On the other hand, a full moon can triple your strength and power," she explained as I slurped on my soup.

"So how do I turn the... 'lunar thingy' off like you did for me today?" I asked. She shrugged.

"The lunar effect can easily be blocked by setting up a blocker. You're basically blocking your receivers, per say. If you can shield your thoughts, you can block everyone else out. Practice, now," she said, pulling my bowl away from me. I sighed and swallowed the last spoonful I took before I did as she asked. I concentrated on blocking her. She studied my face for a moment before she chuckled.

"You have no idea what you're doing, do you?" she asked. I shook my head. "You're focusing on me, focus on yourself. Try to put up an invisible wall around your mind brick by brick for the time being. The more you practice, the easier it'll get over time until you don't even have to think about it anymore. You'll still be able to vibe people's feelings with the blocker, but their thoughts won't intrude upon yours," she instructed. I imagines bricks being set up around my mind in a dome form brick by brick. It was hard to hold on to the image, but I tried to focus on it and put everything else out of my mind. It took a lot of effort and I was mentally exhausted after the ordeal. But Aria just smiled.

"Good. Took you longer than I thought it would, but you did it," she said. "Now keep practicing, tearing the wall down and building it back up," she instructed. Taking the wall down was a lot easier.

"What about the confidence I had today? How did you do that?" I asked, getting sidetracked. She rolled her eyes as her hand dropped from underneath her chin.

"You're barely through the first lesson. And I didn't do anything. I just brought forward the confidence that was already inside of- great, you're making me sound like a damn Hallmark card," she said as she hopped off the stool. I chuckled at how right she was. It was like listening to the end of a Christmas movie.

"Seriously, what was it?" I asked.

"I just blew off some of the timid crumbs to expose your connection to the badass Moon Goddess inside of you," she explained. I still didn't get it.

"How do I do that on my own?" I asked. She smirked.

"This is an easy one. Just pull my essence towards you. Think of how much of a badass I am and channel it to use it to your advantage. You're connected to the Moon Goddess. Be humbled, but don't be a wimp," she instructed. I tried to think of what she was saying but it was harder than simply building a wall. This was about changing the way I felt about myself. I had to chant a mantra, but eventually I felt a tiny bit of the confidence I had this morning.

"I think I'll just have to keep working on that one," I said unsurely. Aria groaned and rolled her eyes.

"Seriously?! You are literally connected to the creator of your species. That alone should give you the confidence of a thousand suns," she said in irritation. She took a breath as she tried to calm down.

"Okay, okay... every time you feel less than confident, just think, you're the only person who has these powers in the whole world. I haven't done anything like this in a very long time, but I did with you," she said.

"How did that play out anyway? What made you save me?' I asked as I slid my soup back near me and started eating again. She slid her hand down her face.

"Okay, this will be the last question for today from you because I'm getting irritated," she said, giving her disclaimer. She sighed before she sat back down. "I hear the prayers of wolves. I heard the prayers of your mother and father loudest that night, so I took a look at what would have my creatures in such... duress. Your father was praying for me to save his mate, while his mother was praying for you. After your mother ripped her stomach open to get you out, I only had enough time and energy to save one of you. I answered your mother's wish. She had already lived her life and you were just a newborn. Plus, I saw a chance to have a legacy of my own. I can bring wolves away from the brink of death, but bringing a wolf back from the dead leaves a piece of me inside of them; a portion of everything that I am because I essentially become your life force. It's something I cannot play around with. I have to be careful. If my powers go to the wrong person, things could be disastrous.

"You hadn't even taken your first breath yet. Laying there on the table as the nurses frantically tried to decide who to save... I chose you. Then after your mother died, I knew your father wouldn't be able to handle it; he wasn't created to. Seeing his face as he looked from your screaming face to your mother's slumped body, I knew he was ready to end himself, despite the fact that he now had a child to take care of. It was gruesome, that hospital room. I stuck around and kept him alive long enough to raise you. It wasn't easy, hiding all of his pain and suffering from you all of those years. Your father wanted to keep you away from this life forever. I think he thought if he never came back, it would be like none of it ever happened, but you needed to come back. I gave him until your senior year of high school to get you here. You were allowed to know about your wolf lineage, but he chose not to tell you. You're connection to me was to be suppressed until you were surrounded by other wolves who could protect you.... here, with your family and your pack. It was my fail safe to make sure you weren't too cocky about what you can do," she explained. I looked at her confused.

"But you are literally the cockiest person I know," I said slowly, not understanding. If I was supposed to be just like her, shouldn't I be cocky, too?

"Well duh, but you're a wolf, and I'm immortal. You have to be humbled because you can be killed. I don't want the power getting to your head too much," she explained. I heard the door to the house open and a rattling of keys.

"Dani?" my grandma called for me from across the house. I looked at Aria, curious as to what she planned on doing. Would she let my grandparents see her? She perked an eyebrow at me before hopping off of the stool gracefully and placing a kiss on my head.

"You don't need your mate to live like normal wolves. You can actually choose your mate if you wanted, but I'll teach you about that later. Luna Addie is trustworthy enough to confide in, if you wanted to talk to someone other than me. I trust her. I'll be back tomorrow, my child," she said softly before she vanished into thin air with just a trace of white dust.

14. A Confidant

My grandparents rounded the corner just as I placed my bowl in the sink. They were relieved to see me smiling. "Looks like you're still smiling. I'm glad," Grandma Nora said as she hugged me gently. I chuckled and nodded.

"I feel great actually," I answered, "Could you drop me off at the Alpha's house? I need to talk with Luna Addie," I asked. They looked surprised and understandably so. I was willingly going to be around my mate who didn't want me. But he wasn't why I was going, and thanks to Aria, I knew that I didn't follow the typical guidelines for the 'mate: do-or-die' rule. It stung a bit, but it wouldn't kill me.

"I-I'll take you," my grandpa offered. I thanked him before going to grab my coat. In the car, I worked on building up my mental barrier brick by brick until it was in place. It didn't take nearly as long as the first time. I was actually starting to get the hang of it. My grandpa dropped me off and I walked briskly through the cold to go knock on the door.

The temperature was dropping with the evening and I didn't fare well in the cold. The short time I spent outside was enough to make me shiver through my thick coat. Much to my disappointment, Liam was the one who answered the door. He looked shocked to see me.

"Dani, what are you doing here?" he asked shocked. I rolled my eyes as I tried to pull more if my confidence out to the forefront.

"I came to speak with your mom," I said, trying to ignore him. He blinked for a moment as I stood there, shivering. "Is Luna Addie home or not?" I snapped at him. He moved aside and let me in. I released a breath as I moved to warm myself. I shrugged off my coat and hung it on the coat rack near the front door.

"Dani, can we talk for a moment?" he asked. I didn't face him as I headed straight for the living room.

"No, but you can lead me to your mom, or point me in the right direction. I have things to discuss with her," I answered.

"And you can't tell me?" he asked as he stood in front of me. The question was laughable. I couldn't help it when a chuckle escaped. "I'm your mate," he added confused by my reaction. I smiled sweetly and touched his cheek. He relaxed as electricity flowed between us. It felt good, but not good enough to make me forget.

"The only reason you want to talk to me now is because everyone knows the truth, and you're scared... as well you should be," I said to him before patting his cheek and letting go.

"You won't be able to ignore the mate bond forever. It doesn't work that way," he said as he caught my hand in his. I chuckled and released my hand.

"You might not be able to ignore it for long, but I can turn it off completely if I wanted to. It's another perk of being connected to the Moon Goddess," I said with a wink before I took a step back. "I'll find her myself," I said as I turned towards the house. I focused on Luna Addie and felt a pull from her calming demeanor and nurturing spirit. The pull took me up the stairs and to a door. I knocked first and opened the door after being granted entry. Luna Addie was sitting at a desk. She chuckled when she saw my confused expression.

"Lunas have to work, too," she answered my unspoken thoughts. I closed the door behind me and tried to build the walls around the room to keep eavesdroppers from listening. I wasn't sure if it would work, but it was worth a try. "What can I do for you?" she asked.

"I just need someone to talk to. Apparently, I have a connection with the Moon Goddess, Aria, and she's been teaching me these... things, and says I have powers. I needed someone to confide in and she suggested you," I explained. Luna Addie's smile only widened.

"I knew there was something special about you. I'm honored that the Moon Goddess thinks so highly of me," she said.

"She's not really... as depicted in wolf history," I said hesitantly. I told Luna Addie everything, and I started with what Aria told me about my birth. I ended with telling her of my option to break the mate bond with Liam. She was shocked, to say the least. Who your mate was wasn't really a choice for wolves. For a moment, she didn't say anything.

"Do you want to break the bond?" she asked. I shrugged.

"I don't know. He's done nothing but deny and ignore me since he discovered who I was to him, but now..."

"Everyone knows that he's been lying. Does anyone know it's you?" she asked. I shook my head.

"I don't think so. I figured if he actually cared-"

"He would tell everyone on his own," she finished for me. "And he's still said nothing," she guessed. I nodded. She sighed heavily. I knew this was hard for her because it would mean that her son would be without a mate. And being the next in line for Alpha that would mean the pack would go without a Luna. She was trying her best to remain impartial.

"It's your call. If you feel he isn't worthy, then he isn't worthy," she said. "Whoever your mate will be, they will have to be strong and understanding," she added. I chuckled softly.

"That's not what you wanted to say," I said. She only shrugged.

"Regardless of my personal involvement, it's the truth, and I can't be selfish," she said honestly.

"It's not selfish. It's your job to worry about your pack. I appreciate that," I countered.

"I know this isn't easy for you, having everything thrown on you like this within the last month alone. If it were me, I would probably still be freaking out. You're very brave and blessed to be trained by such a feared goddess," she said. I shrugged.

"She's teaching me a few things, but she's actually more normal and... vain than you would expect," I said with a chuckle.

"I suppose that's a good thing," Luna Addie said with a smile. "Well, I'm here if you need anything. And I'll respect the confidentiality... even from my son," she assured me.

"Thank you," I said as I stood. I turned to the door and took a deep breath before breaking the walls down around the room and putting them back up around my thoughts. Luna Addie stopped me as she stood beside me. She hesitated before she held her hand out, palm up towards me.

May I?" she asked. I nodded before setting the wall back up around the room and taking my mental one down. I took a breath before I placed my hand in hers.

I gasped as the images hit me. It was my mother. Luna Addie and my mother were in a hospital room with my father. My mother was in labor with me. I saw everything through Luna Addie's eyes. She was encouraging my mother to push, along with my father. The monitors spiked suddenly. Nurses rushed around the room as the doctor tried to make sense of what was happening. He told my mother they needed to prep her for a c-section because they lost my heartbeat. They overheard a nurse say that they might not get to me in time. That's when my mother took matters into her own hands and used her claws to rip open her own stomach, gritting her teeth the whole time. The doctor stood there shocked for a moment before my mother's hazed eyes went to his.

"Save her," she ordered. The doctor took me out of her stomach and immediately took me over to the table to begin CPR. They fussed over me as tears sprung to my mother's eyes. After a moment, her heartbeat started to slow. Luna Addie held my mother's hand in her own tightly.

"Stay awake Beck!" Addie urged her. My mom turned her head to look at my father.

"You take care of her. Take care of Daniella. You have to promise me that you'll see her till her senior year. You cannot leave her. Do you understand me, Robert?" my mother said to my father, her words slurring slightly. He was crying.

"No, you're going to be here to watch her grow up, too," my father said through his tears. The nurses came back to my mother but she refused the help.

"Save my baby," she whispered hoarsely. My father wasn't having it.

"No, Rebecca, stay awake," he begged.

"I love you," she whispered before her eyes slipped close and the monitor flat-lined. The nurses and midwives were confused as they moved between my mom and I. My dad was crying for my mother to wake up. Luna Addie didn't know what to do as she felt the heartbreak of her friend dying, but she know she had to at least try to honor my mother's last wish. Before she could touch me, I started screaming. Once Luna Addie got me to calm down, my eyes opened.

Glowing a mix of silver and blue.

She knew, in that moment, that I was special in some way, but when she went to check on my father and me the next day, we were gone, and there was no scent to follow. I had a sneaking suspicion that that's when Aria arrived disguised as Evelyn.

I released the Luna's hand with a gasp and was thrown back into reality. I was panting, trying to catch my breath as the haze began to fade. I felt tears leaking down my cheeks.

"Thank you," I said softly as I wiped my face dry.

"Did you want to stay for dinner?" she asked at the same time my stomach growled. "I know about being a vegetarian," she explained quickly. I hesitated. On one hand, I was starving and food sounded amazing right now. But on the other hand there was Liam. Food trumped any other issue automatically with how hungry I felt. I smiled at her.

"I would love to," I agreed.

15. Dinner with the Millers

The dinner table was awkward to say the least. Liam was watching my every move carefully, Alpha Conner was trying to tiptoe around my eating habits, Bella was glaring at me from across the table, Lily just wanted to eat her food quickly so she could get back to playing with her dolls, Luna Addie was ignoring everyone's weirdness and keeping up a table-wide conversation with minimal input, and me? I was trying to ignore the fact that this whole thing was slightly uncomfortable. There was a tension that hung in the air that I couldn't ignore.

"Have you ever eaten meat before?" Alpha Connor finally asked. I nodded and decided that the truth was the quickest way to get him to drop it.

"I was tied up and force-fed semi raw chicken after watching it murdered, and fed whatever I threw up in the process until I kept it all down," I said calmly before taking another bite of the delicious garlic bread. The table was quiet as they all stared at me.

"So sorry you had to go through that," Luna Addie sympathized, breaking the silence. I shrugged.

"It was necessary at the time," I said, meeting Luna Addie's eye. She seemed to understand it had something to do with my powers.

"Dani," Liam started.

"Don't talk," I said shortly, cutting him off.

"You can't talk to my brother that way!" Bella growled at me in his defense. I raised an eyebrow in amusement.

"She can, Bella, and you shouldn't stick your nose up at things you have no knowledge of," Luna Addie snapped at her.

"Why are you taking her side? Why is she even here? When Sophia finds out about this-"

"Sophia isn't my mate, Bella!" Liam blurted as he stood. He sighed and bowed his head in shame as his eyes glued themselves to the table. "Dani is," he admitted. I couldn't help the glare that burned through him.

"That's for me to decide and I'm not so sure of that right now," I said as he finally met my eye. They table was quiet ans the tension around us thickened. I sighed as I stood, keeping my eyes on his shocked expression. "You don't get to call me that until you earn it... if you earn it, and at this point in time, I'm tempted to break the bond completely," I explained. I took a breath before I looked at the rest of the table's confused and shocked expressions.

"Dinner was delicious, Luna Addie," I thanked her softly. She stood and gave me a gentle smile as if the whole thing never happened.

"Of course, dear. I'll drive you home," she offered.

"Thank you," I said fleetingly as I went to grab my coat from the front. I met her in the garage as she grabbed a pair of keys and headed for the SUV. The car ride was easy and wasn't nearly as awkward as dinner was as we rode in peace. After dropping me off with a goodbye, I rushed into the warmth of the house and out of the cold as I shut the door behind me. I released a breath and relaxed.

"Dani?" my grandmother called.

"Yeah, it's me," I yelled back before I started heading up the stairs to my room. I knew they had questions but they gave me my space. I shed my coat to the floor and turned on my portable heating unit my grandparents got for me. I showered and got ready for bed quickly. I wasn't in the best of spirits after dinner with Liam, but I wasn't hurting either. I was more annoyed than anything else. It helped knowing the ball was in my court and Liam would just have to wait and see.

I wasn't ready to fully give up on him just yet, but I was still bitter that he was so passive about me in the first place. The pull must not have been that strong for him if he could pretend that I didn't exist. When I stepped back into my room, Aria was sitting on my bed. I jumped in surprise before I tried to calm my racing heart.

"Could you give me a warning before you just show up?" I asked. She chuckled with a smirk.

"Literally, no, but you'll get used to it," she shrugged. "Good on you for sticking up for yourself tonight. Feisty... I like it," she said as she stood. I sighed and threw on my pajamas.

"I'm really tired, Aria," I said.

"Okay, go to bed then. But Liam is going to kiss you tomorrow," she said. I froze before looking at her. I couldn't see any part of what happened tonight urging him to even be around me at the moment.

"I won't let it happen," I said. She chuckled as I pulled the cover to my bed back.

"You need to let it happen. You won't be able to stop it anyway. Just be prepared. A mate's kiss isn't like anything you've ever felt before," she advised.

"Why are you telling me this?" I asked confused as I got in my bed, keeping my eyes on her.

"So the ball stays in your court, and so you don't dodge it. You need to let it happen to understand," she said with a wink.

"You were listening to my thoughts," I said as I sat up. She shrugged.

"What part of 'connected' don't you get? You're an open book to me, and sometimes I get bored," she replied. I laid my head back on the pillow and I adjusted on my side.

"I don't mean to be," I said. She sat on the edge of my bed and gently moved my hair back.

"It's not a bad thing; just means I raised you right," she said with a sad smile. "It wasn't how I wanted your childhood to be. I never wanted you to see me as a monster. I wanted you to laugh and just... be a child. After all, you're the closest thing I've ever had to a daughter, but your own safety was more important. People would kill to get their hands on you. Packs could use you to start a war. I had to make sure they didn't know you existed, and suppressing your powers was the only way to make sure of that. I'm sorry, for how you viewed me growing up, but I did it because I love you... and you are technically an extension of me," she said. I sighed and got comfortable as she played with my hair. It was weird, I thought I would hate her more, but I understood where she was coming from and why she did what she did. It wasn't out of spite; it was out of love.

"I forgive you for... everything. Oddly, I understand," I said out loud. She smiled.

"Get some sleep, you're going to have a long day tomorrow. I'm going to start training you myself; what you need to learn, your school can't teach you. And you need to build up your strength. You should start eating meat again," she said before placing a kiss on my cheek and disappearing.

She was a little unorthodox, yes, but she was technically the closest thing I had to a mother, and a craved that. She did bring me back to life. She was looking out for me and my best interest like a real mother would. I didn't understand when I was younger, but now knowing the whole story, I understood. She was trying to protect me.

If I were an Alpha and I knew someone could predict danger and heal people with a direct line to the Moon Goddess, I would want them on my side, too. I hadn't exactly been secretive about my connection with Aria. I'd have to be more careful. Hopefully, word wouldn't get around too fast because I still had a lot to learn to protect myself.

16. Busy Moon Goddess

The next day at school was pretty calm, but it felt like the eye of a hurricane. It was a brief calm in the middle of chaos and I knew it. I was on my toes for Liam due to Aria's words of warning. Aria made it seem like it was important that I let it happen, but there was no way in hell I'd let Liam get away with a move like that after everything he'd done so far. Mya was happy to see me as I walked to my locker. She was wary of if I was going to explode in fear or sass, but happy to see me nonetheless.

"Hey," she greeted me. I felt Liam's eyes on my back I glanced only long enough to see that he was alone. No Sophia in sight. He passed and I released a breath, turning back to my locker.

"What is up with you two? You've been at it like cats and dogs since you met," she asked. I shrugged.

"That was just the aftermath of a very awkward dinner," I explained. Her eyes widened.

"You went to the Alpha's house? You had dinner with his family? Sophia never even sat with them for dinner," she said. I only shrugged.

"Luna Addie was a close friend of my mother's before she died. We talked for a bit and then she invited me to dinner," I said dismissively. "We're going to be late for class," I said as I closed my locker. Mya silently agreed with me as we parted ways and went to our respective classes. I sat away from Liam, conscious of his thoughts. They were thoughts of longing and regret.

Good.

Not even five minutes into the class, I was called into the principal's office. I made my way there curiously, unsure of what was going on. When I got inside, I saw a pale, white-haired figure floating opposite of the room from a very flushed and fearful-looking Principal Scotchman.

"Aria," I said in amusement. She smiled back at me.

"My child," she replied; her voice changed to sound like an angelic echo. "I was just explaining to your principal how you'll be leaving school to study under me from now on," she said. I wanted to laugh at this because it was so different from the Aria I knew, but I kept my mouth shut as I bowed my head briefly.

"I'll go gather my things," I said eagerly. I was trying to prevent the kiss from ever happening. She shook her head as she smirked at me knowingly.

"You will be free to leave after certain events have occurred," she said before placing a kiss on my head.

"You've got to be kidding me," I deadpanned. Principal Scotchman looked scared for me while Aria only laughed; her goddess-like laugh sounding like clear chimes.

"I will see you when you return home," she said before a bright light soaked her up and the room was normal again. She was gone. My principal was shaking in his seat as he finally plopped down in the chair behind his desk. He looked at his desk, not knowing what to do, so I left and went back to class. I slid back into my seat right before the bell rang. When it did, I tried to leave quickly, but unfortunately, Liam caught up to me.

"What was that about?" he asked. I shrugged.

"I'm being pulled from school," I answered simply as I kept walking.

"What? Why?" he asked, getting angry. I smirked, keeping my eyes forward.

"Aria thought my studies would be better learned under her guidance. What I need to learn, this school can't teach," I answered. He stopped me from walking any further by standing in front of me; putting us at a standstill in the middle of the hallway.

"Why is the Moon Goddess so interested in you?" he asked accusingly. My lips quirked in amusement.

"Surely you didn't think any of what I could do was by chance, did you? You had to know something was different about me. Or were you too concerned about what other people would think if you were seen talking to me?" I shot back at him.

"I'm not embarrassed of you. I'm embarrassed of myself," he admitted reluctantly. I scoffed before trying to step around him.

"Whatever," I muttered. I felt it the anticipation of nerves coming off of him in waves, but I couldn't place what it was for. Everything seemed to slow down as he pulled me back to face him and pushed his soft lips against mine. Time seemed to stop as sparks flew and seemed the tingle through my body. My body felt like it was completely under his control. I felt breathless as my heart started pounding in overtime. I was completely frozen. It was like nothing I'd ever felt before. Aria tried to warn me, but I underestimated the power of the mate bond. I greatly underestimated what Liam's touch could actually do to me. I should have known better.

I did know better.

I pushed him away to put space between us. By now, everyone stopped in shock as they watched us. Despite myself, my vision blurred. My reflex was to slap him, which is exactly what I did. I should have been better prepared. But then again, I'd never been kissed before ever; let alone by my mate. I didn't know what to expect, but now I knew. Liam had somehow gotten ahold of my wrist. His eyes searched mine, willing me to listen. I knew what his words would be before he even opened his mouth, but I didn't stop him this time. I didn't trust my own voice.

"I am truly sorry, Dani. I never meant to hurt you. I was a coward. Please... let's just start over," he begged. I kept the distance between us as I took a shaky breath.

"I-I need time... to think," I said quietly, trying to get a little privacy from the curious eyes. "Don't follow me," I added before I turned and went to my locker. I grabbed my things, leaving all of my books, and headed towards the front of the school.

"Hey! Where are you going?" Mya asked, jogging behind me to keep up.

"Home. I never should have come today. I knew this was going to happen. She told me so and just let it!" I ranted angrily, and mainly to myself. Mya stopped me in the parking lot. I took a breath, creating a visible cloud in front of my face as the cold hit me like the end of an ice whip.

"You're Liam's mate... that's how you knew Sophia was a fake. And he was just going to go along with it?" she realized. I hesitated before letting out a sigh.

"I really just need to go home right now," I said softly. She quickly pulled out her keys.

"I'll take you," she offered. I gladly followed her to the car. Inside, she blasted the heat for me and my teeth chattering began to subside. "I'm sorry," she said as she drove. I only shrugged.

"I really don't want to take about it," I said as I looked at the passing scenery out the window. The rest of the ride was quiet except for the occasional directions. She parked in front of my house with a heavy sigh.

"I'll see you tomorrow?" she asked unsurely. I sighed myself before I shook my head.

"Aria pulled me out of school. I won't be going there anymore," I answered.

"That sounds like... such an honor," she said, shell-shocked. I shrugged.

"Sometimes... sometimes it's a burden too," I muttered to myself. "I'll call you later though," I offered. We shared a quick goodbye before I rushed inside to warmth. Going to the living room, I was met by my grandparents and Aria in her wolf-depicted form from the principal's office.

"You sure have been busy today," I said a bit bitterly as I dropped my bag on the couch. My grandparents' eyes budged at my brashness.

"Daniella, manners!" my grandma said out of fear of what Aria would do in retaliation. My grandma was about to apologize for me but Aria just laughed.

"You're acting more and more like me every day. Come on, let's get started with your lessons," she said as she glided past me and out the door. I took a breath before I followed her, grabbing a scarf for extra warmth on the way out.

17. Lessons

I walked quickly after Aria into the nearby wooded area. I watched her back angrily as we did so. Slowly, her glowing white figure morphed into the red-headed Aria that I grew to know. Her feet landing on the ground as she began walking instead of floating. Finally, she stopped abruptly, making me run into her and stumble back a few steps.

"Why did you let that happen?" I asked angrily. She sighed and rolled her eyes. She could have pretended she didn't know what I was talking about, but that would've been a waste of both of our time.

"I wanted you to know a portion of what the mate bond feels like. You were numb to the effects compared to Liam, and, although he's an idiot, you didn't understand either... not completely anyway. You still don't. But I think you have a better idea now of what the mate bond truly feels like. It's special. I want you to be fully aware of the consequences before throwing it away out of spite," she explained.

Why not just tell me?" I asked with a shake of my head.

"You may have believed me, but you wouldn't know what it felt like until you felt it for yourself. It's not something I can describe to you. It's not something I experience. He's still a boy, Dani. He has a lot of growing up to do," she explained. I sighed and ran my hands over my arms to try and get some heat back.

"Why are we outside?" I asked. Her hand raised beside her in a short arch as she whispered something to herself. It was suddenly comfortably warm. I relaxed, only a touch, as I waited for Aria to speak.

"Nature is a force and source of energy for us... well another one. When the moon is new, you will be weaker, as you now know. You can make up for it a little bit by drawing from the Earth's energy. It still won't be enough to make you feel one hundred percent, but it'll be enough to get you through the day without passing out like you did last time," she explained before she sunk to her knees in the dirt. "Do as I do," she said. I went to my knees as well, curious about where she was going with this. I mirrored Aria as she pressed her hands into the ground, took a deep breath and closed her eyes.

"Try to feel the movement under the Earth; the flow of energy," she instructed. I took a deep breath and focused as she said. It took a moment but I finally found the invisible stream under the hard dirt. A small smile graced my lips at my minor accomplishment. I felt slightly recharged.

"That was... relaxing," I said as I sat back and enjoyed having my guard down. She chuckled.

"Well, you stress too much anyway. It's a nice charge on a new moon, but the moon will have you stronger than Earth on any given day. Full moons will nearly triple everything about you from vision to power," she explained. I sighed as my smile fell and my thoughts drifted back to Liam.

"You shouldn't let him consume your thoughts," she said knowingly. I couldn't help it after that kiss. Thinking about everything simultaneously made my head spin with questions.

"But I don't know what to do about it... or him. I felt it in every nerve of my body when he kissed me, but... he wants Sophia. And I'm not going to be his second choice," I said defiantly.

"He wanted her... but no regular wolf can resist the mate bond. They can try but it'll eventually drive them mad until they can't think about anything else. He literally can't take a breath without thinking about you. Stubborn at first, but I told you: he's a boy. He hasn't quite matured, but he realizes the fault in his mistake. He's trying to make amends. It's the only way to ease his soul and keep from going completely mad and bloodthirsty. Denying a mate, can turn a wolf insane, literally. It's rude to deny a gift from a Goddess, and there is a price to pay for doing so. It would be wise to forgive and show your maturity. You don't want to see what happens to a wolf who's denied a mate," she said. I knew she was probably right, but I still wanted to hold on to my grudge because I was hurt.

"I'm not saying to accept him with open arms, just talk to him. You can have another mate, but he only gets you. And without you, he'll turn feral," she reminded me.

"I wouldn't even know what to say to him," I breathed.

"Just say whatever comes to mind. Be truthful. Some wolves will kill themselves before going feral. He literally wouldn't be able to live without you. He feels even worse because he knows that it's no one's fault but his own," she explained.

'What are you in his head or something?" I asked. I she nodded. I sighed heavily. I didn't want him to kill himself by any means, I was still so angry though.

"What's next on the lesson plan?" I asked, trying to change the subject. I didn't want to think about Liam anymore. She sighed before she stood.

"You know what; you need to go see him tonight," she said.

"Can I give him time to stew? He only acknowledged wo I was to him today," I said with a bit of a whine.

"Don't be spiteful. He acknowledged you and pushed his own embarrassment aside. The longer you wait, the worse he'll get. Go see him, even if it's just to tell him that you don't hate him. And I know you don't," she ordered.

"I don't need a guy. I've been fine on my own so far," I argued in frustration. She shook her head.

"You're a demi-goddess first, a wolf second, but still a wolf by nature. You will need a mate, period. It's been that way since the beginning. You just have more of me in you than I originally thought. You're not entirely immune to the bond, but not completely destroyed by it either. You're only hurt," she said. I groaned as my head went back slightly.

"Why are you pushing this so hard?" I asked. Her eyes narrowed at me slightly. I guess she wasn't used to people questioning her.

"I have my reasons. I was okay with you teasing him a little, but you're being completely irrational now and playing with his life," she said. "I'll meet you in your room for your next lesson," she said before she disappeared. The heat went with her. I shivered before getting up quickly and retracing my steps back to the house. It was a good thing we weren't far or I would've been lost. I went to my room and saw Aria was already there as her white figure.

"Glamour," she said simply.

"What?" I asked confused, and still pissed from my cold walk. She whispered something before turning back to her normal red-haired self.

"Glamour; it's the act of changing you r appearance or anything really so it appears different to other people. Clothes, face, hair, anything. Just think about what you want to change and how you want to look. Be as specific as you can and just focus," she instructed. I took a breath and closed my eyes as I focused on my hair. I thought of changing it to my father's dirty blonde color with his straight hair and honey accents. I focused hard and cleared my mind of everything else.

"Good, not link your fingers together and say 'with a knot'," she instructed. I did as she said and repeated her words. I opened my eyes and went to look at myself in the mirror. I touched my hair in shock to see it was the exact color of my father's. "Now to undo it, just link your fingers back together and say 'untie' as she let go," she said. I did it and watched as my hair changed back to its natural, black color right before my eyes. I blinked as I just stared at my reflection.

"H-How?" I asked confused. She whispered something under her breath before she touched my arm. I gasped at myself in the mirror. I was still me, but everything seemed to be glowing. My eyes looked brighter and more iridescent. My hair looked smoother and a darker hue of black. My skin was clearer. I looked... beautiful. My clothes were changed too. I was in a bright blue, V-neck sweater and cropped blue jeans with gray ankle boots. I touched the mirror in shock, unsure of the way I looked. She tied it off and looked at me approvingly.

"There, now go see your mate," she said. My eyes bulged.

"You want me to go like this?!" I asked in shock. She only smirked.

"Just trust me," she said. I shook my head.

"I hope toying with my love life won't become a regular thing with you," I said unamused. She only hugged me. When she let go, we were outside of the Miller's house. Then she dissolved with the next gust of wind.

"Go easy on him," her voice whispered in the wind. I was left standing there with two options: risk freezing to death and walk home, or go to the door.

I sighed and faced the house as the cold stung my cheeks. I was going to have to find a way to get Aria back for this stunt.

18. Sorry is Just a Word

I went to the door before I knocked hesitantly. The door swung open and revealed Bella. She was surprised and conflicted to see me. She wasn't sure how she felt about me anymore. She hated me because she thought I was trying to take her brother away from his mate, but now... she wasn't sure of anything, and she didn't trust her brother. She was in awe of my appearance though.

"Can I speak with Liam?" I asked calmly. She moved aside and held the door open more without saying anything. She was embarrassed of herself too. I went to where I knew his room was and walked in without knocking. He was sitting with his head in his hands on the edge of his bed. He slouched and I could feel the defeat and self-loathing radiating off of him like heat waves. I could sense that he was torturing himself, and it made me feel guilty for a moment.

"Liam," I sighed empathetically. He looked at me shocked. He was so out of it, he didn't even notice me come in. His eyes were red and slightly puffy.

"W-What are you doing here?" he asked, standing quickly. His jaw dropped slightly as he looked me over in shock. "You look... different," he said hesitantly. I shrugged.

"Aria's doing," I dismissed it. "You look miserable," I said jokingly. A very small, almost unnoticeable, smile touched his lips for a quick second before he was serious again.

"I'm so sorry, Dani," he apologized. But he seemed sorrier of his own suffering. I sighed and took a step away from him as he took a step forward.

"You still don't get it, do you?" I asked. "All I wanted was for you to look at me like I was actually your mate. You did, once, in the beginning, but afterwards, I was your burden. I was your secret and shame. You didn't want anything to do with me. I shouldn't have had to be the one to tell the truth for you. I shouldn't have had to out your fake mate for you to finally tell the truth about her. And even then, you still didn't acknowledge me. You only kissed me out of guilt because you felt bad and got scared when you heard I was being pulled from school. No more looking at me when you thought no one was watching. No more ignoring me in front of your friends, but also trying to discreetly watch my every move. You realized that I would be gone and out of your vision and reach. And you finally felt bad after weeks. The funny thing is, I don't need you. It won't destroy me or make me feral if you deny me for the rest of my life. Yes, I was hurt, it was a gut-reaction that can't be helped, but I'm not required to need you to survive. You, however, do need me or you will go feral, and you know it. And then who's going to run the pack? For someone who had so much to lose, you didn't play your cards well," I said, speaking whatever came to mind like Aria suggested.

"What do you mean by 'you don't need me'? I'm still your mate," he asked as he sat back on the edge if his bed, his eyes still trained on me.

"Exactly what I said. I have more of Aria in me than wolf. The Moon Goddess doesn't need a mate, and I'm similar. I can choose anyone as my mate. You're not my only option. A mate for me is more of a comfort instead of a need,' I tried to explain.

"So to me, you're my mate in every sense of the word, but to you... I'm just optional company?" he asked, trying to wrap his head around what I was telling him. I nodded with a slight shrug. He sighed and shook his head.

"That doesn't seem fair to me," he said in frustration. I shrugged.

"It's not, but based on how you've treated me up to this point, I'd say it was a blessing in disguise. If I were a normal wolf, someone emotionally weaker, I would have been destroyed by your betrayal. And you would have been without a mate by your own doing anyway," I replied.

"I said I was sorry," he reminded me. I chuckled but the situation was anything but funny.

"You only apologized because you're lonely now and you've been made by your peers. If you could have kept pretending with Sophia, I would have still been an afterthought to you," I countered.

"If you're not here to forgive me, why are you here?" he asked.

"I didn't really have a choice. Aria dropped me at your front door and said I should try to understand what the mate bond really feels like," I explained, trying to choose my words carefully. He sighed and ran his hands down his face.

"So you're saying that you don't know half of what I'm feeling right now?" he asked. I shrugged because I honestly didn't know. He took a heavy breath before he stood in front of me and held out his hand. He looked at me expectantly. I knew what he wanted, but I wasn't sure if I wanted to know. Eventually, I gave in and took the wall down before taking his hand.

I gasped as everything went black. I was intrigued and curious as to what I would see this time. I tried to focus solely on Liam's feelings. It went back to the beginning. I was us, but everything was mute this time. I just felt what Liam was feeling at the time. I was left completely breathless the first time Liam was me. It was like the wind was knocked out of me. His chest was filled completely and his body was set aflame as the breathless feeling subsided. When he touched me for the first time, every nerve was buzzing. It was like he hadn't actually taken a full deep breath in his whole life until he saw me.

The scene skipped forward to when I passed out in the woods. He was worried. He paced and watched me as every bad scenario flew through his mind and caused an aching in his chest. When I told him I didn't need him at dinner, the hollowness came back tenfold, followed by an intense aching pain that just wouldn't go away. Fast forward to when he kissed me in the hallway. It was similar to what I originally felt but extremely more intense. It was nearly paralyzing. I couldn't take the rollercoaster anymore. I had to let go.

I gasped as I turned away from him with the urge to clutch my chest. It felt like I was about to have a heart attack. Compared to what he was feeling, what I felt was muted. What I felt was a gentle breeze while Liam's was a hurricane. I wanted to hold him and comfort him, but so many questions popped into my mind, stopping me. I closed my eyes for a moment, trying to calm my breathing, heart, and thoughts. He was quiet as he just waited. The overwhelming amount of emotions made my eyes water, but I held back the wannabe tears. When I opened my eyes, I was even more confused and angry than I was before.

"If that's how you felt, how could you even think of denying me? How could you pretend like I never even existed after all of that?" I asked as angry tears replaced the ones of sympathy. He looked at his feet as he rubbed the back of his neck nervously.

"I was a coward... I was scared. You were new. You knew nothing of what we are, and I already told everyone that Sophia was my mate. Going back and saying 'just kidding, I lied' as a future Alpha is embarrassing," he said. I shook my head.

"What I just felt could easily cancel out any embarrassment that would've come afterwards. You would have to just have not wanted me at all to try and ignore everything you felt," I said. I could feel him getting antsy as I watched him get frustrated.

"It's more complicated than that," he tried to defend himself. I shook my head.

"It's really not," I argued. "If you felt that intensely, why waste your time fighting-" I stopped as his thoughts rolled into my head like they were my own. He didn't speak, but he didn't have to. I caught it all. Focusing on him, I saw it all clearer without even having to touch him. It was always there, I just misinterpreted it incorrectly.

"You're afraid of me," I said in realization.

"Was; I was afraid of you at first. What is are... I've never seen anything like it. It's not so easy to swallow and I still don't understand it. But now I don't care. You're my mate first and most importantly. That's all I can think about now. You have literally consumed my thoughts. Whatever else you can do, I'll just have to accept it. You're perfect the way you are. We were made for each other, and I should have never done what I did to you. I know that now. If I could go back and start over, I would. I would beg on my knees everyday if it meant that you would one day forgive me and keep me as a mate," he said quickly. I could sense that he completely meant what he said. He was beyond sorry. Guilt flooded his conscious.

"I know what's in your heart. You don't have to beg," I stopped him. He was too sorry to be afraid of me anymore...

But he should've been.

19. Progress

"Where do we go from here?" Liam asked softly. I took a deep breath and shrugged.

"I don't know," I answered honestly.

"Are you rejecting me as your mate?" he asked hesitantly. I shrugged.

"I don't know," I repeated. "But I could use a ride home," I said. He nodded and grabbed a jacket as my invisible wall went back up. We headed to the garage. We were both quiet as Liam drove but it didn't feel like a goodbye. Other than the occasional directions, neither of us said a word the entire ride. When he parked the car in front of my house, he looked at me longingly. I tried to ignore it but it was nearly impossible in this small enclosed space.

"Can I come see you tomorrow?" he asked. I hesitated before I nodded. I promised I would give him another chance, but I wasn't ready to jump into anything with him. We would be taking it at a snail's pace for sure. But I had to at least continue talking to him face to face in order for that to happen. As much as I wanted to hate him and move on with my life, I had to listen to Aria and give him one last chance.

"Sure. I'll text you," I agreed. We swapped numbers before I got out of the car and walked briskly through the cold to the warmth of the house. My grandparents were lounging in the living room and watching TV.

"How was your day?" my grandpa asked when they saw me. I shrugged.

"Fine," I answered as I took a seat on the couch. "A lot to adjust to," I added for their benefit. They didn't press any further, but I doubt they ever would. They were just happy to have me in their lives again.

"Will you be joining us for dinner?" my grandma asked. I nodded.

"I don't see why not," I replied. I'd been so busy trying to figure everything out with Liam and dealing with Aria that I often skipped dinner. In fact, I hadn't been spending much time with my grandparents at all lately. And after everything they'd done for me, taking me in, no questions asked, I owed them to try and get to know them better.

"I'm sorry for my absence lately," I apologized. They were quick to wave me off.

"You're a special girl, Danny. We understand that your plate has been a tad full lately. It's not your fault," my grandma assured me. I hugged her gently.

"Thanks, I'm going to shower," I dismissed myself. I sprinted up to my room and wasn't surprised in the slightest to see Aria sitting on my bed in her red-headed form.

"That was a lot of 'I don't knows' with Liam," she noted. I was not looking forward to this conversation at all.

"I'm not a 'forgive and forget' type of person. That's as good as it's going to get for now," I defended myself. She sighed before shaking her head.

"I should have never told you about the chosen mate option," she muttered to herself. "Look, I misread him initially. He is trying. You're being hard on him," she said to me.

"But I'm technically you, right? What would you have done if your mate rejected you for weeks?" I asked.

"Well, firstly, I would kill for a mate. I don't get to have the companionship of another where I go. I'm constantly looking over the wolves, I can't be distracted. It's a lonely job," she answered longingly. "But we're not talking about me. He was wrong, yes, but I'm just asking you to have a little more... empathy," she said. I picked out some long johns and grabbed my towel.

"Empathy isn't my thing. You taught me that. Goodnight, Aria," I said, heading towards the bathroom.

"Whatever. I'll see you tomorrow," she said before she vanished. I was pretty sure I pissed her off. I got ready for bed before going down for dinner with my grandparents. Tomorrow was going to be better. Or at least, that's what I was trying to will myself to believe.

~

"Healing draws from you own life force so you'll need to be careful with it. Too much and it'll kill you," Aria warned me during my lesson. For the first half of the day, we were doing some air-bender type moves straight out of the cartoon Avatar, but Aria said it was called Tai Chi. She said it would put me in the right state of mind before teaching me how to heal.

"Like everything else, it's about the right state of mind. You focus and will it to happen; pulling from inside yourself," she instructed. We were knelt over a deer that was laying with a cut on its back leg. Aria moved my hand over the wound and instructed me to start. I focused on closing up the wound. It took nearly twenty minutes as Aria kept the deer calm, but it finally closed, leaving a small scar in its place. I stopped and slumped back on my heels with a yawn. I was exhausted.

"Good, good. Practice and it'll get easier. With time, you'll get stronger and it won't take as much of a toll on you. Of course, this was a very minor heal. You shouldn't try anything bigger than a cut until you come into your wolf. Like healing, you can also hurt someone too. Try to reverse it. Create a cut," she instructed. I took a breath and dug my hands into the earth as I felt for the current of energy. When I finally found it, I drew from it to reenergize myself before trying to reverse what I healed. Aria kept the deer calm and still as I worked. It was much easier to open the wound then it was to heal it.

"Why was that easier?" I asked.

"Causing pain requires you to draw from your own hurt and anger... and you have a lot of it. To hurt someone else, you project your own onto them," she explained. I sighed and sat back to pull more energy from the earth. I was getting lightheaded. I sighed and sat back as Aria healed up the dear in less than a minute and released it.

"So when do I shift?" I asked. She sighed and crossed her legs.

"Normal wolves shift between ages 7-12. The stronger the wolf, the sooner they shift. Those people tend to be more in touch with their animalistic side. You almost shifted at the age of 3. I had to suppress your wolf for a while. You weren't ready. I will give her back when you're ready. When she comes, you'll be immensely stronger than any wolf ever born," she warned. "You won't be able to pull her out whenever you want either. Your human form is stronger. Your wolf will come out when it shows to be an advantage for you, or when she feels like it," she added. I sighed heavily.

"At what point do I get a normal moment?" I asked sarcastically. She chuckled.

"It's a burden sometimes; I won't deny that, but you're alive," she reminded me. I sighed as my thoughts drifted to Liam. I was supposed to meet with him today after school got out and it was nearing that time. I wasn't going to lie, it was making me anxious.

"You're thinking about him," she noted. I nodded. It was pointless to try and hide it from her, she was in my head.

"I wish I knew what to do," I admitted.

"Now that you've felt the true intensity of the bond, you want that, but you're still scared he'll go back to her," Aria spoke my deepest thoughts out loud.

"But... I know what I saw," I defended myself.

"Your vision? The vision was fulfilled already. Your visions aren't long term. You haven't gotten that advanced yet," she shook her head at me before sighing heavily. "What you saw already came to pass. Once a vision is fulfilled, that's it. You saw him choose Sophia, and he did. Now it's over, and it's time to move on," she explained.

"I don't trust him," I said.

"Yes you do," she countered. "He's going to need you, and believe it or not, you're going to need him. You've gotten even, now it's time to humble yourself," she said.

"I really don't want to get hurt again," I admitted.

"You're more powerful than he is, my daughter. He fears more than you do. He'll keep your secrets, out of fear if nothing else," she promised. She stood and helped me to my feet before opening her arms for me. I sighed, knowing she was about to drop me off at his door. I held her and closed my eyes briefly as a gust of wind landed me right in front of his house. She tucked my hair behind my ear with a smile before taking a step back.

"Try to have fun today," she said before vanishing. I took a deep breath before I knocked on the door.

20. Fake Fresh Start

B ella was the one to answer the door. The corner of her mouth perked in an unsure smile as she moved aside to let me in.

"Hey Dani. Liam is in his room," she said. I smiled warmly at her.

"Thanks, Bella," I said as I shed my coat and hung it on the coat rack near the door. Lily ran up to me with the biggest smile as she hung on my arms.

"So are you Liam's new girlfriend now?" she asked excitedly. Her innocence was adorable. It made me giggle as Bella rolled her eyes and tried to pull her back a bit. Lily protested and Bella eventually gave up.

"No, I'm not, but let's go find him," I smiled at her. She nodded before darting ahead of me up the stairs. I chuckled as I followed her. Seeing Lily made me long for the childhood I never got. I went down the hallway and to Liam's open door. Lily was sitting on Liam's bed next to him, kicking her feet absentmindedly as she looked at him. Upon my arrival, her attention veered to me.

"I found him!" she said excitedly. I crossed my arms and leaned against the doorframe.

"Go see if Mom needs any help with dinner," Liam said to Lily. She hopped up and raced out of the room. "Hey," he greeted me.

"Hey yourself," I replied, walking further into the room.

"So did you meet with the... Moon Goddess today? That is so weird to say out loud," he asked. I nodded as I sat next to him.

"You can just call her Aria, its fine. And yes I did. I'm exhausted," I answered. He looked at me confused.

"Why did you come here then?" he asked.

"A promise is a promise," I muttered as I curled up on my side with a yawn. "Plus, Aria dropped me off at your door so I didn't really have a choice," I added truthfully.

"You could take a nap here. I mean, if you wanted to. I could stay, or leave, or you could go to a different room if you want. Or-"

"Liam," I stopped him. This is fine, really. I can take a quick nap here," I said. As tired as I was, I would just be cranky the whole time anyway. Liam pulled off my shoes before pulling the covers back. I crawled under and rested my head on the pillow as another yawn escaped me.

"I'll let you sleep," he said softly. I closed my eyes and fell asleep almost immediately.

~

I woke feeling groggy but a warm, comforting feeling spread through my body from my arm. I looked over to see Liam shaking me away gently.

"What happened?" I asked, confused.

"My mom wanted me to wake you. She made dinner and wanted to make sure you ate," he explained. I sat up and yawned as I stretched.

"Okay, I'll be right down," I said, still feeling tired. He hesitated before he left me alone. I sighed and ran my hands down my face. Resisting him would be harder to continue when he was being sweet like this. It was easier when he was an asshole. I would have to be adamant about taking this slowly. Not that I was ready to jump into his arms or anything, but this was a good start.

After freshening up a bit in the bathroom, I went down to the dining room where Liam's family was waiting. Luna Addie smiled when she saw me.

"Dani, have a seat. I made zucchini pasta," she said. I thanked her as Liam handed me a plate with food. Alpha Connor's plate was still piled high with meat, but that was to be expected. It was his nature. I ate quietly, lost in my own thoughts, as the table interacted with each other. Liam's glances didn't go unnoticed. It was like he was being extra careful not to try and scare me away.

"Do you think you'll be going back to high school at some point?" Alpha Connor asked me, pulling me into the table's conversation.

"I'm not sure, but I don't think so. Aria doesn't really give me a heads up on her plans. I just kind of go along with them but I've got a lot to learn from her and I feel like we haven't even really started," I replied.

"Is she every bit as beautiful and amazing as we're told?" Bella asked excitedly. I chuckled with a shrug.

"She is very beautiful, and she knows it. She can be full of herself but it's warranted, and she means well. She doesn't really need to be... down to earth," I joked, picking my words carefully. Luna Addie caught the joke and laughed.

"It would seem so," Luna Addie said. We ate and talked and it was actually really nice. As far as family dinners go, I didn't really have many growing up, and the one I had with the Millers before ended a little awkwardly, but this was fun. It was nice. After dinner, Liam drove me home. I hesitated as we sat in the car in front of my house.

"I actually didn't hate today," I said, trying hard not to make it sound too much like a compliment.

"Good enough to nap over at my place again?" he asked jokingly, but I could hear the underlying seriousness behind his words. I chuckled before I nodded.

"Yeah, we'll see," I said. "But let's actually use texting this time. Aria dropping me off at the front door is going to get tiring really fast," I thought out loud.

"We could go out for lunch or something," he suggested. I chuckled before hopping out of his car.

"I'll see you later," I said before closing the door and going inside. I could smell the chicken and dumplings as soon as the front door closed behind me. The smell itself smelled delicious, but the thought of the chicken immediately made me nauseous. "Smells good," I said, heading for the kitchen. I figured my grandma was whipping something up.

"I thought so," Aria answered as she turned and set a bowl on the counter. I was confused. I was a little shocked that she had actually cooked.

"What is this?" I asked hesitantly. She set a spoon down before taking the pot off of the burner.

"You're not going to like this, but you need to start eating meat again. I know the 'whole chicken spell' kind of ruined it for you, but you're going to need your strength. And when your wolf comes, she's going to want meat. And if she doesn't get it from you, she'll find it on her own, and you do not want her killing anyone for it," she explained. I sighed as I stared at the steaming bowl in front of me. "Oh come on, there's barely any in there," she whined. I scrunched my nose up at the food as I tried to get myself to take a bite.

"Why did you start with chicken?" I asked, finally looking at her as I realized I couldn't bring myself to do it. She rolled her eyes as she huffed out a breath.

"Oh my god," she breathed. "Chicken is what ruined meat for you so it's best to start with it so the others will come easier. Just trust me. You're wolf is too strong to survive on a vegetarian diet. She'll get meat one way or another, and you'll want to eat it when it's cooked. I don't even have to tell you how raw meat can do a number on your stomach," she explained further. I sighed and put a little on the tip of the spoon. I hesitated before bringing it to my lips and putting it on the tip of my tongue. It wasn't even enough to swallow. I looked at Aria expectantly. I thought I would've gagged or thrown up or something, but nothing happened. I still didn't want to try pushing it.

"There, happy?" I asked. She sighed and sat next to me at the bar.

"It's a start at least," she gave up.

21. Like a Normal Teenager

Saying things were going slow with Liam was an understatement. I just couldn't shake feeling like the other woman that quickly. It still lingered. I hung out with Mya a lot. This particular day Mya took me out to the local mall. I hadn't gone out to anywhere in weeks so it was nice to get out. We met up with Kaden and Taylor. After walking around and grabbing a few things, we went to the food court. I was in the mood for Chinese and ice cream. We sat as we talked and ate. It was nice to hang out with people my age and not worry about Liam or Aria for a little bit.

They didn't invite Liam to hang out with us because they didn't want it to be awkward. Last they heard, I ran away from him after he kissed me in the hallway. I never really gave anyone an update on the status of Liam and me, and I really didn't want to. I also didn't tell Liam about hanging out with his friends because frankly, it was none of his business who I hung out with in my spare time. Sophia wasn't invited for obvious reasons. If she came around wielding her attitude like a weapon with me, I would get a chance to practice my newfound skills, and I wouldn't be trying to heal her.

"So how has it been not going to school? Sounds like a good deal," Kaden asked. I shrugged.

"I wish it were as easy as you're making it sound," I chuckled. "I still get up in the morning and have lessons. It's just not math and science," I explained vaguely.

"Still... it must be cool hanging out with the Moon Goddess all day. Have you talked to Liam lately?" Mya tried to ask nonchalantly.

"Well she is my mate," I heard an answer from behind me before I could. My cheeks heated red being caught off guard as he sat next to me.

"Hey," he greeted me.

"What are you doing here?" I asked. I wasn't trying to be rude, I just wasn't expecting him. I briefly wondered if he lo-jacked my phone to keep track of me. But I never let him touch my phone so that thought was thrown out as quickly as it entered.

"Bella and Lily wanted to go somewhere, and I decided to give my mom a break so here I am," he answered. "Hey guys," he greeted the group. They were drinking up the scene. I could hear the questions they thought and could see the confusion on their faces but they wisely kept their mouths shut.

"Dani!" Lily said excitedly before crawling into my lap. I chuckled and settled her before giving her the rest of my ice cream.

"Hey Dani," Bella said as she walked up coolly.

"What are you doing here?" Liam asked me as he pulled Lily off of my lap and onto her own seat.

"Socializing," I said smartly.

"I didn't know that," he pouted slightly.

"You're not entitled to my every move," I retorted with a playful smirk. He rolled his eyes with a sigh.

"Are you coming to the bash tomorrow?" he asked. I wasn't even aware that a party was going on. I looked at Mya and Kaden confused.

"Pack Bash. It's like a big barbeque/social thing," Mya explained.

"Well, seeing that this is the first I'm hearing of it... no," I deadpanned.

"Sorry, with everything else going on, I forgot to tell you. I guess I just kind of assumed you would come," he explained apologetically.

"You should know better than to assume anything," I reminded him.

"So will you come?" he asked. I thought about it.

"A crowd of people with food, outside in the cold... sounds like a swell time," I said sarcastically. Everyone at the table just stared at me. I finally caved with a roll of my eyes. "Fine, I'll think about it," I said reluctantly. Liam smiled and hesitated slightly. He wanted to kiss me. I gave him a look of warning as I watched him. Giving him a look that clearly said 'don't'. Even if I were that comfortable with him, which I wasn't, I hated PDA.

"The dress is casual," he said before plucking Lily from her seat and walking off with his sisters as they waved goodbye to me.

"Well that was... unexpected," Mya said honestly. I bet they were expecting a yelling match or at least more hostile banter. I shrugged.

"We've communicated a few times," I downplayed it.

"You didn't bite his head off," Mya corrected me. I couldn't help but to laugh at it and they were laughing just as hard as I was. It was comical to be honest. Now that I had possible plans for tomorrow, Mya decided that it called for a new outfit specific to the party. Taylor and Kaden were tired of shopping around with us so they went to the arcade.

Mya dragged me into a few stores we passed up on the first round of shopping. She picked out a gray knit sweater dress that hugged my shape and ended a little past my knees. It had a simple neckline and long sleeves. It was simple, but pretty. She paired the dress with knee-high black boots. It definitely wasn't what I had in mind when Liam said 'casual wear'.

"Mya, he said casual. One, I'll be overdressed, and two, I'm going to freeze my ass off," I said to her, looking at the outfit in the mirror.

"Yeah, Liam says casual, but Luna Addie really means 'classy', you know? Guys always mess up fashion unless they're metro. The party is outside and I know you get cold easily, but you're also the future Luna. Trust me," she tried to assure me. Despite my protests, Mya bought the outfit for me, and a skirt, sweater combo for herself. She was full of energy and excitement and mine was starting to waiver. I felt freezing cold and slightly out of breath by the time we reached the arcade.

"Are you okay?" Mya asked, slightly worried. I leaned against the nearby wall as I tried to catch my breath.

"I-I'm fine," I lied.

"The new moon is getting closer, so you're weakening" Aria's voice filtered through my thoughts like a gentle wind. I rolled my eyes.

"And you didn't think to mention that before now?" I asked out loud.

"What?" Mya asked. I shook my head.

"Nothing, I was... I should go home soon," I dismissed it. I had to learn how to stop answering Aria out loud when she does that so I didn't look so crazy. After finding the guys and dragging them away from the games, we left the mall. Mya dropped me off at my house before she drove off, promising to come help me get ready tomorrow... if I even decided to go. I had to say, I was a little nervous. I'd seen some of the kids at school the short time I was there and I knew the Alpha family, but I hadn't met the whole pack. Especially not all at once. And I had a feeling Liam was going to do something I definitely wouldn't like. Now with the new moon approaching too, I just wanted to crawl into my bed and sleep for the next 24 hours. I threw my window open and leaned against the window sea as I took a deep breath of the fresh, crisp air.

"Feeling a little weak?" Aria asked. I took another breath before I turned to face her.

"Like I might pass out at any minute," I answered, watching the darkening sky.

"You should go outside. Root yourself to the earth," she suggested. "The new moon is tomorrow and you'll need your energy for the party," she added.

"I'm not going," I said, making up my mind. Aria groaned.

"Why not?" she whined.

"I'm too weak, for one. And two, I hate large crowds anyway," I explained.

"You're going, and it'll be outside so you'll be fine. You know how to pull energy from the roots of a tree so you won't even have to get into the dirt and mess up your outfit," she said. I let out a dissatisfied breath and turned to face her.

"But-"

"You're going," she said before she disappeared. I groaned before plopping down on my bed.

Stupid Moon Goddess...

22. Not An Ammend

I smoothed my hands over the dress as Mya looked me over. She came over a few hours ago to force me to get ready. She was already dressed by the time she sat me down in the bathroom to straighten my hair. She was subtle with the makeup she put on me before forcing me into the dress.

"I think it's even more perfect than before," she said with a huge smile. I looked myself over in the mirror. I couldn't help but to think of how much I looked like my mother. Mya squeezed my hand gently.

"Ready?" she asked. I nodded.

"Yeah, I just need to grab my stuff. I'll meet you at the car," I said. She left my room and I hurried to my closet to change into black ankle boots, jeans and a red sweater. There was no way I was wearing that dress today. I slid my phone into my pocket and grabbed my keys. I got in the car and Mya frowned at me.

"You changed," she noted.

"We're going to be late," I smiled at her. She rolled her eyes before Mya drove us to the Alpha's house and we went straight to the backyard. There were already hundreds of people talking and laughing with each other.

There was a long table full of food and the Alpha family stood slightly elevated on the small hill near the tree line. Liam spotted me almost immediately. He smiled before making his way to me.

This is stupid, I thought to Aria. I knew she was watching, whether she made herself known or not at the moment.

"You made it," Liam said happily. I shrugged.

"Well I didn't really have a choice," I muttered behind my forced smile.

"You look great," he said as his eyes swept over my body.

"Thanks," I said uncomfortably. Liam himself looked like a clean cut model. He was wearing a simple white button up with the sleeves rolled up and the top button loose and khaki slacks.

"Come on," he said, taking my hand. He took me with him to where his family were standing on the hill.

"What are you doing, Liam?" I asked, too late. Luna Addie smiled and hugged me.

"Dani! So glad you could make it," she greeted me.

"Excuse me everyone! Your attention please," Liam addressed the crowd. They hushed as they looked at him. I stayed near Luna Addie, not wanting to draw attention to myself.

"As you all probably know by now, our retired Beta's granddaughter has returned to the pack. What you may not know is that she is also my mate," he announced. My eyes went wide as a hushed murmur spread throughout the crowd.

"Are you insane?" I hissed at him. He looked at me and reached to grab me but I glared at him and took a step back. "Touch me and you die," I warned.

He blushed as his face went to one of shock before he recovered and left me.

"So let's give Dani a warm pack welcome," he finished. The crowd clapped and hooted but I could tell that behind the noise, there was mostly confusion. The crowd went back to their previous conversations as Luna Addie chuckled and put an arm around my shoulders.

"Sorry sweetie," she apologized.

"What was that?" I asked Liam as he walked the short distance back to us.

"All new members are introduced," he said smugly. I knew they weren't introduced like that, and he knew it too.

"You know I can hurt you without even touching you right?" I reminded him. He chuckled nervously before turning into a conversation with his father. I felt a wave of weakness hit me and pressed my hand against a nearby tree to pull energy from. The leaves on the tree all turned brown as they died almost instantly. I took the moment to walk down the hill to where the rest of the crowd was eating and talking amongst each other. Liam followed behind me.

"What are you doing?" I asked as I stopped to face him.

"Mingling?" he said questioningly.

"Go mingle over there. I'm going to find Mya," I chuckled. He sulked but stopped following me and I continued on my mission to find my friend. I was stopped many times and given hugs and welcomes by strangers which slowed me down a bit. Well, that and the fact that I was weak from the new moon.

"Welcome to the pack," someone said sarcastically. I was hoping she wouldn't have come at all, but no such luck. I turned to see a very pissed off looking Sophia.

"Thank you," I replied with a plastered smile. I was in no mood to play games with her today.

"Oh, and good luck... you're going to need it," she muttered.

"What is that supposed to mean?" I asked, turning my attention back to her. She shrugged in mock innocence.

"It's just that you're kind of... replaceable, right?" she asked. I chuckled and relaxed.

"No, not really. Last time I checked, you were the replaceable one, remember?" I said, mocking her.

"We'll see," she said, looking up the hill to where the Alpha Family was.

"I guess we will," I said before I continued to look for Mya. I finally found her by the punch bowl. I sighed in relief.

"I have literally been looking everywhere for you," I said as I leaned against the table.

"I haven't left the food," she giggled. "I wasn't expecting Liam to introduce you like that," she said. I sighed and nodded before I settled for pouring myself some punch.

"You're telling me," I muttered before I took a sip. I felt him before I saw him.

"Aren't you supposed to be mingling on the other side of the field, Liam?" I asked without turning around.

"I tried, but you're over here," he said cheekily as I sipped on my punch. I wanted to get inside his head but there were too many people here, and I hadn't quite mastered singling out one thought with a crowd this big. And taking my wall down now would just overload me. I was working on it though. Liam wrapped an arm around me, almost making me spill my punch. Mya jumped in and took the cup from my hand.

"You're not going to ruin her outfit. Even if it's not the one I picked for her," she said, setting the cup on the table. Liam chuckled before he moved to kiss me, I turned my head and pushed out of his grasp. We hadn't kissed since that one time at the high school, and I wasn't about to start in front of everyone in the pack.

"Liam," I warned. His smile was still easygoing.

"Relax, Dani. It's just a kiss," he said. I glared at him.

"I already told you how I feel about that, and I expect you to respect my choices. Just because you finally decided to publicly claim me without asking in the first place doesn't mean that I'll suddenly start acting like a love-struck fool," I ranted. "We are going at my pace," I reminded him. He sighed and all but rolled his eyes.

"It's been weeks," he whined.

"My pace, and I say not yet," I countered. We were starting to draw a few onlookers. Mya looked between the two of us before looping her arm with mine.

"We're just going to go to the ladies' room for a moment. Dani isn't feeling well. We'll be back," she said quickly before dragging me out of the crowd that was starting to get a little too nosy. We went inside the center and straight to the bathroom, as promised.

"I know you are in charge and whatnot, but you should really be careful where you decide to express your 'strong independent woman' remarks. I know you don't care, but the pack is sworn to protect the Alpha Family if someone defies them. Even if it's a future Alpha's mate," she warned. I groaned and rolled my eyes.

"I just hate how he tries to use the crowd to manipulate me. I'm not going to be all over Liam. I hate PDA for one, and he hasn't earned a damn thing more, either," I ranted.

"I know, but they don't. Typically, finding your mate equates to instant babies within the next few months, but I know that your circumstances aren't the same. The pack will only see that you're not following tradition. You'll be questioned for not accepting the role of Luna and carrying Liam's pups. They'll see you as thinking you're too good for him and the pack. I know it's frustrating and annoying and not at all fair, but it's all they know, and right now, you're challenging that which makes you the enemy," Mya tried to explain. Of course, I knew all of that, but I refused to compromise my self-worth for a stupid tradition.

"Of course... you could always do what I would do and just tell them to go screw themselves. But that's not very becoming of a Luna, is it?" Aria input her two cents as she sat perched on the counter with her legs crossed as she examined her nails. Mya jumped backwards in surprise as she gasped.

23. Unexpected Visitor

"I thought you didn't pop in with others around in this form?" I asked, raising an eyebrow at her. Mya stared at my red-headed version of Aria in shock. Aria shrugged as she tossed her hair over her shoulder.

"Eh, I like Mya. You trust her; I trust her. Plus she fears me too much to say anything, and rightfully so," Aria explained.

"I wasn't expecting you until tonight. What changed?" I asked.

"Watching you piss off a pack is fun, but Sophia is up to something, and I plan on doing something about it. I would suggest you do something, but the whole moon thing, and this problem requires my delicate touch," she explained. I glanced at Mya who was still staring at Aria like she was a ghost.

"Don't worry, she'll snap out of it eventually," Aria waved it off.

"So what's so important that I need your help?" I asked, getting back to the subject at hand.

"Sophia is going to try something stupid, and it's easier to tie up her hands instead of wasting your energy," she said vaguely.

"I thought you didn't medal in petty wolf affairs," I asked.

"I don't, but this is different. She's messing with your life, and inadvertently messing with me. And no one embarrasses me, ever," she answered. I figured that was all I was going to get out of her for now.

"Y-You're the Moon Goddess," Mya said, finally snapping out of it. Aria chuckled.

"That, I am, Mya," Aria confirmed before hopping off of the counter. I checked my hair in the mirror and reapplied some chap stick.

"Y-You know my name," Mya said, still shell shocked. I didn't want to burst Mya's bubble and tell her that Aria knew everyone's name, but it earned a chuckle from me.

"Just keep being a good friend to Dani," Aria said to Mya as she touched her shoulder gently. Mya went into a shocked state again as she stood there frozen.

"What did you do to her?" I asked knowingly.

"I just gave her a little good luck. Nothing to worry about," Aria said innocently. "Oh, and stop being so harsh to Liam, at least in public. You're like Cruella, and the pack is watching you closely now," she said before she vanished. I sighed as I leaned against the sink.

"That was the Moon Goddess," Mya said innocently. I chuckled and shook my head as I looked at her. She didn't seem noticeably different to me, which was good.

"Are you going to be okay?" I asked. She nodded excitedly.

"That was the Moon Goddess," she repeated with a big smile. I was about to suggest we get back to the party, but screams erupted from outside followed by growling. Mya and I looked at each other before we rushed outside. The kids were being herded inside the building as we stepped back out into the chill. I maneuvered to the front of the crowd before an arm held me back. I looked to see Liam as he pulled me into his side. I allowed it as I looked at what was setting everyone on edge. Two rogues had stumbled into the field and it looked like we missed all the fun. One rogue was slayed out on his stomach with gashing wounds running down his back. The other rogue was on his knees with his neck extended in a sign of surrender. Alpha Connor stood closest to the rogues with his hand covered in blood. It was probably from the rogue.

"You picked a hell of a day to wander here, kid," Alpha Connor said to the rogues. They looked around my age, if not a little bit older. Sophia seemed to move forward out of nowhere as if someone were pushing her against her will. Mya did next. They looked at the rogues and froze instantly.

"Mate," they said almost at the same time. Everyone heard them and knew what it meant.

"These rogues are your mates?" Alpha Connor asked for verification. They nodded without looking at Alpha Connor. I noticed the injured one looked like he was about to bleed out. His face was going pale.

The injured one is Sophia's mate. Heal him now, or he's going to die, but don't overdo it, Aria whispered in my head. I wanted to groan out loud but I kept it in. After a reluctant second and an eye roll, I moved forward as well.

"Alpha, may I suggest some... privacy? If we don't get the injured one help, he will die," I suggested, my eyes on the ground out of respect. He nodded before ordering everyone else away. The only people who stayed were Alpha Connor, Luna Addie, Liam, Mya, Sophia, and myself. Sophia rushed to move her mate.

"Don't touch him," I ordered. She turned to growl at me. I rolled my eyes. "If you move him, he'll die for sure," I explained.

"What can you do that I can't?" she challenged.

"Well, I can heal him, for starters," I shrugged as I moved towards them.

"You're lying. We need to get him to the healer," Sophia said to me, before talking to Luna Addie.

"Actually, Dani is your best bet," Luna Addie stuck up for me. Sophia sighed before she backed up. The other rogue was already up and holding Mya. She looked so happy. I got on my knees over the injured rogue who was now coughing on him own blood. I pressed my hands against the hard dirt first and focused, pulling the energy from the earth before I touched either side of the rogue's gash. He yelped quickly, which earned a growl from Sophia. Alpha Connor, held her back after that. I focused on the rogue and felt the energy drain from me as the wound started closing up. I could feel his organs shift and mend under my fingers. He screamed as I healed him. I continued until I felt myself start to get dizzy, and a trickle of blood ran out of my nose.

"Okay, that's enough," Liam said, stopping me. I looked up, feeling light-headed. I sat back on my butt with a breath. The rogue was now sleeping peacefully. Liam scooped me up and placed me on my feet. I swayed slightly. Liam held me upright. "Are you okay?" he asked.

"I-I need to lay down," I breathed. Sophia moved to her mate and touched his face gently.

"What's wrong with him? I swear if you hurt him I'll-"

"She saved your mate. I think the words you're looking for are 'thank you'," Alpha Connor stopped Sophia's rant. Mya's mate looked at me.

"Thank you... for saving my brother," the other rogue thanked me. I was about to say 'you're welcome' when everything started to get spotty.

Damn it, Aria.

24. Rogues

I woke with a headache. I groaned as I slowly opened my eyes to a dark room. I was in Liam's room. I sighed and just relaxed as I laid there. I was tired still. I felt drained. I felt a hand on my head.

"You're awake," Liam said softly.

"Yup," I said, popping the 'p' at the end. "Did you just watch me the whole time I was out?" I asked. He shrugged.

"Had to make sure you were still breathing," he explained. I sighed before I sat up with a grunt. Liam tried to help but I waved him off.

"Will you open a window?" I asked. He jumped up quickly and threw the window open. I took a deep breath as the crisp air rolled through the room. "How's the injured rogue?" I asked. Liam moved to sit beside me again.

"He's alive... paralyzed, but alive," Liam explained. I thought about healing him more when I was stronger tomorrow.

No, that's enough. The new moon is still out and you've already done more than you were supposed to. Leave him, Aria said to me. I rolled my eyes. So that was her plan? Give Sophia a mate that she'd have to wait on hand and foot? It was evil... it was genius. Sophia would definitely have her hands tied doing everything for her mate. Oh Moon Goddess you work in mysterious ways.

"Help me get outside," I said to Liam. He cradled me and carried me easily without question. Once we reached the front door, he stopped.

"Now what?" he asked.

"Set me down in the forest," I answered. He let out a sigh before he began walking towards the trees. It was incredibly dark out, but I could see easily.

"I hope that there's a purpose to this," Liam said more to himself than to me as he stopped in a clearing and set me on my feet. I carefully laid down on the ground with my palms pressed flat into the earth. It was chilly, but I welcomed the burst of energy the wind brought. I sighed and relaxed as I felt the energy return to my body.

"I can pull energy from the earth. You can't tell anyone, but new moons weaken me," I explained with my eyes closed. I felt Liam sit beside me.

"Is that like a recent thing?" he asked. I released a breath before I shrugged.

"Since I found out who I really am," I answered. It was peaceful and quiet for a moment before I felt Liam lay beside me.

"Do you still hate me?" he asked. I thought for a moment before I sat up and looked at him. His eyes were already trained on me.

"I don't hate you," I answered. "I was disappointed and hurt and first. Then I was angry, and now I'm just... seeing where it goes," I added.

"Why won't you kiss me then?" he asked. I chuckled as I looked at the stars for a moment.

"Because of when you want to kiss me. It's always public, like you're trying to prove a point. It doesn't feel sincere; rather territorial. But if you tried to kiss me in a setting like this, where we're alone, I would be less inclined to stop you," I explained. There was a good tension in the air as his eyes met mine. He leaned forward slightly and I felt myself doing the same. We were only centimeters apart.

"Liam?! Are you out here?" Luna Addie called from the front door. He stopped and closed his eyes for a second with a breath of frustration before sitting back again.

"Yeah, mom. Dani wanted to go outside," he answered.

"We should go check on that injured rogue," I said, standing. Liam stood as well and we walked back to where Luna Addie was waiting by the door. She smiled warmly at us.

"It's dark out and with the recent rogue incident, your dad doesn't want to take any chances," Luna Addie said to Liam.

"It was my fault. I needed to reenergize," I apologized. "Can we go see the rogue?" I asked. Luna Addie hesitated.

"He's... not what you would expect," she tried to reason. I looked at Liam confused. He just shrugged.

"It's okay. mom," Liam said. She sighed before grabbing her coat.

"Alright," she said, heading towards the garage. We got in the SUV and she drove us to the infirmary. It seemed to still be busy despite the late hour. After checking in with the front desk, we went to the waiting room to wait to be called back. Mya and her mate were in there. I smiled at her immediately and hugged her.

"Hey," I greeted her. She looked like she hadn't stopped smiling since the incident in the field.

"Hey yourself," she chuckled. She moved back to stand beside her mate. "This is my mate, Carson," she introduced him. I smiled and shook his hand.

"Nice to officially meet you," I greeted him.

"Likewise," he chuckled. "I owe you a huge 'thank you' for saving my brother. Anything I can do, please let me know," he added. I waved him off.

"How is he doing?" I asked. Carson averted his eyes for a moment.

"He's... alive, but he's not taking the news of his state well," Carson explained. A nurse came into the room and smiled politely at us.

"You can see him now," she informed us. I turned back to Carson.

"I guess I'll see for myself," I joked. Liam and I followed the nurse back to a room. Immediately walking in, Sophia was sitting by his bedside with a remote in her hand while the rogue laid in the bed.

"No, no, no, no, no," he was saying as Sophia flipped through channels for him. She looked slightly annoyed. They stopped when they saw us.

"How are you feeling?" I asked, trying to break the awkward silence.

"Well let's see, I can't feel anything from the neck down. I'm paralyzed," he retorted. I blinked in surprise. Such an attitude for someone who was just on the brink of death.

"Well at least you're not dead," Liam defended me.

"Can you heal Clay again like you did in the field to make him not paralyzed?" Sophia asked. Ah, so his name was Clay. I shook my head.

"I can't," I answered. Her eyes narrowed at me.

"You can't, or you don't want to? This is you trying to get back at me, isn't it? You're still mad that I was with Liam first and he chose me over you," she snapped. Liam growled at her to back down.

"I chose my pride, not you specifically. And if it wasn't for Dani, you're mate would be dead right now, but I'm not going to let her kill herself over it. He's alive. That's all that matters. Be grateful you're not turning feral," he stopped her.

"Thank you for saving me to live a life where I can't do anything for myself," Clay said sarcastically. It was evident that they were both crawling under Liam's skin. He looked about ready to pop a blood vessel. I touched him gently to calm him down.

"You're welcome," I replied anyway. He rolled his eyes before turning his attention to Sophia.

"Go get me water. I'm thirsty. And none of that warm crap either. Use ice this time... and a straw," he ordered her. She sighed before she got up and went to the little serving area in the room. Liam and I turned and left. I couldn't help the smile that cracked through. Clay and Sophia were absolutely perfect for each other.

25. You and Me

It was oddly silent with Sophia's hand's tied up with Clay, but it was nice. Mya was gone spending time with her mate as well. Aria backed off to give me time to get to know Liam better. And Liam... Liam was still walking on eggshells. And thankfully, it was finally starting to warm up.

"Ready?" Liam asked. We were going on a picnic. And thankfully, Aria taught me how to make myself warmer, so I wasn't too worried about the tiny leftover bite in the air. We walked the short distance from his home to a clearing where he already had a blanket set out. He set the basket down and we sat as well. Liam even went out of his way to make cream cheese and cucumber sandwiches for me. Aria was still pushing for me to eat meat again but I only tried one other time and it didn't go too well. I'd gotten in the habit of showing Liam things Aria had taught me and practicing in front of him.

"How has school been?" I asked him. He shrugged.

"It's okay," he brushed it off. "I miss seeing you all day, though," he added. I chuckled and rolled my eyes.

"I promise, you'll live," I replied, putting the empty baggy back in the basket and taking a sip of water. I formed my hands around an invisible ball and circulated the wind in my tiny atmosphere. It was something new I had been working on.

"How are your grandparents doing?" he asked.

"They're good," I said, temporarily distracted by my tiny wind tunnel. I made it slightly bigger before letting it go. I smiled before pecking him on the cheek. I'd been getting pretty bold lately with Liam. I was comfortable with him, and I accepted him as my mate. We hadn't kissed again, officially, but little pecks here and there were acceptable. His face lit up as he pulled me closer to him and pressed his lips against mine. I didn't fight him or pull away. I let it happen, knowing it was long overdue. My hand moved to his cheek as I deepened out kiss. His arm wrapped around my waist as he pulled me onto his lap. Butterflies attacked my stomach. When I felt like I couldn't breath anymore, I finally pulled away. He was grinning from ear to ear.

"I love you," he said gently. I could tell he meant it with every fiber in his being. I wasn't ready to say it back yet, but we were getting there. I pecked his cheek.

"We're getting there," I replied. I could feel the overwhelming love rolling off of him. He wasn't upset or hurt, just happy.

"I'm glad you gave me a chance. Well, another one," he joked. I could only shrug.

"You should be thanking Aria. She's the one who kept dropping me off at your house unannounced," I laughed. He chuckled and shook his head as he relaxed back onto his hand with his other arm still wrapped around my waist.

"How's the meat-eating going?" he asked. I sighed and rested my head on his shoulder.

"Still tough. I know it's necessary if I ever want to see my wolf, but I just... I can't keep it down. The first little taste was fine but I never actually had to chew anything. The second time..." I drifted off. Aria made a ham sandwich for me one day and had me take an unwilling bite. I threw up almost immediately.

"I don't want to see you hurt anyone. I can help if you want," he offered. I only sighed.

"I know it's something that needs to happen but I just can't bring myself to keep any of the meat down. I don't know if that will change with my wolf," I admitted.

"Well you have less than a month until you figure it out," he reminded me. My birthday was less than a month away. I was turning 18 and Aria was going to unleash Sahria, my wolf. Typically wolves were not granted names, but apparently, mine did. And she sounded destructive. Typically, werewolves were highly in touch with their wolves and could communicate with them and call on them any time they pleased. Sahria and I would be different. I wouldn't be able to call her out whenever I wanted. She would be powerful, but I would have more skills and powers to my use as a human. She would be more for protection in case of emergencies after my first shift. I wouldn't be able to communicate with her and she would choose when it was necessary to make an appearance. She would also choose to make an appearance if she wasn't get enough food, which is why Aria was trying to get me to eat me again before she arrived. Because she was coming whether I was ready or not, and I was not ready.

"I'm actually scared of Sahria," I admitted to Liam. He sighed and kissed my head.

"We have more reason to fear her than you do. She'll protect you," he tried to assured me.

"That's what I'm afraid of," I replied. I was afraid of Sahria going on a rampage and hurting people. This was my pack.I didn't want to hurt anyone in it.

"I'm sure Aria won't let that happen. That's why she's trying to help you eat meat now," he tried to assure me. I sighed and sat up.

"We should go back," I sighed. I moved to lay in the grass and dug my fingers into the Earth, pulling the energy from the ground. I'd gotten so good at that little trick, that I would leave a circle of dead plants when I was done. I enjoyed the energy boost, even when it wasn't a full moon. It was like a high. Liam packed up our belongings before we walked the short distance back to his house.

"Danni!" Lily said before jumping into my arms. That was another thing; Lily absolutely loved me. And I loved her.

"Hello, little bug," I smiled before kissing her head. I set her back on her feet before moving into the living room. Luna Addie smiled when she saw me.

"Danni, how was your picnic?" she asked. I smiled back warmly.

"It was good," I answered. Liam was only two steps behind me.

"Hey mom," he greeter her before he went to sit on the couch, taking me by my hand and bringing me with him in the process.

"Hi honey," she greeted back. Things had calmed down with Liam's family and me a lot. Even Bella and I were getting along great.

"Don't forget that I'm going to be going over to Danni's for dinner tonight," Liam reminded his mom. For the 6 months that Liam and I had been mates, I hadn't allowed him to come over. But since things had been going smoothly for a while, I figured it was time for the family dinner to be on my side of the street this time. Although deep down, I wished he were actually meeting my parents and not my grandparents. And I wished that we had both gotten a chance to meet my mom, Rebecca.

26. Dinner with the Wilders

I didn't make it a habit to try and eat meat at the dinner table in front of anyone on the off chance that I had to throw it up again. Liam was nervous, I could sense that much, and I think my grandparents could too. He was polite and trying to be helpful, but he was talking too much. It was actually kind of cute. He really wanted them to like him, which was silly because they already did. He helped my grandma set up the table and pulled my chair out for me when it was time to sit. My grandma made vegetarian spaghetti. It was obvious the men at the table wanted meat in it, but they didn't complain.

"So Liam, how is your family?" my grandpa asked.

"They're good. Lily is about to start first grade the next school cycle and she can't stop talking about it," he chuckled. From there, Liam relaxed a bit and we mored into easy dinner conversation. I finally got a handle on reading thoughts one at a time so I didn't get overwhelmed in crowds or groups of people. My grandma was still thinking about how handsome Liam was and how much he looked like Alpha Connor. My grandpa was still confused as to how I wasn't craving meat yet. And Liam? Liam just wanted this to go well, and he wanted me to love him back.

After dinner, our little party moved to the living room where the conversation continued. It was pleasant and relaxed. Liam was still slightly worried that my grandparents were being nice because he was the future Alpha, but he really had nothing to worry about. When my grandparents got tried, they said their goodbyes and went off to their room. I couldn't stop smiling at him as he released a breath.

"You had nothing to be nervous about," I tried to put his mind at ease. He chuckled with a shrug.

"The real test will be with your dad," he joked. At the mention of my dad, I got a sinking feeling in the pit of my stomach; like something was wrong. The nightmare I had when I first arrived to this town entered my memory before a quick vision of a lake defrosting in a time-lapse glazed over my vision. "Danni? Danni, what's wrong?" Liam asked, pulling me out of the vision. I couldn't put my finger on it, but something felt wrong.

"Is there a lake around here, near a road?" I asked him out of curiosity. His eyebrows knit together in confusion before he nodded slightly.

"Yeah, there's one on the road leading out of town. Why?" he asked, even more confused than he was before. I didn't understand my abilities at the time, but now that I did, I suspected my nightmare was more than just a nightmare. All I could do was pray that my dad say my text saying that I loved him before he drove into the river.

"Will you take me there tomorrow?" I asked.

"Is everything okay, Danni?" he asked, taking my hand in his. I sighed as a single tear escaped my eye. I tried not to look at him, knowing that it would only cause me to get even more upset than I already was. In my heart, I knew it was true. He didn't have his mate, Aria, or me to keep him grounded. He had kept his promise to my mother.

"I don't think you'll have to worry too much about getting my dad to like you," I answered vaguely. Liam moved to pull me closer to him, but I stood and got distance between us before he could. I was comfortable with Liam. He was my mate and I trusted him, but if he embraced me, I knew I would start sobbing, and I never wanted anyone to see me that vulnerable, ever; no matter who they were.

"I'll see you tomorrow then," I said, quickly wiping my tears away. Liam stood in front of me and held my cheeks gently in his hands until I was looking at him.

"Danni... talk to me, please," he practically begged. Another tear escaped my eye and Liam brushed it away with his thumb.

"Liam, I really don't want you to see me like this. Please go," I said as I tried to choke back a sob. It was like a lump was stuck in my throat and I couldn't breathe. I wanted to talk to Aria and have her confirm my suspicions, but I knew that wouldn't happen while Liam was around.

"Danni, that's what I'm here for. I'm supposed to be the one person you can break down in front of if you need to," he said. I could tell he was getting frustrated but he was still trying to be gentle with me. "Please, tell me what's running through that head of yours," he asked as he moved a strand of hair behind my ear. I closed my eyes with a shaking breath. Hesitantly, I pressed my open palm against his temple. I felt the energy flowing from my hand to his mind. Unwillingly, I thought about that nightmare again. As it rolled through my memory, it presented itself to him.

Showing my visions to someone else through touch was something I rolled my eyes at when Aria taught it to me, but now, with the lump choking back the words I was afraid to speak out loud, it was the only way I could get Liam to understand. After it was over, Liam's hand dropped from my face as he pulled me into a hug. I couldn't help the sob the broke its way out of my throat.

"Oh Danni," he breathed into my hair. I clung to him as I buried my head into his chest. "I'm so sorry," he whispered. I tried to pull myself together. I took a step back and tried to wipe my face.

"Liam you should go," I said, composing myself.

"No, if you need me-"

"No really, Liam... it's okay. I'm just going to talk to Aria before going to bed. I'll call you if I need you, I promise. And I'll see you tomorrow. You can come first thing, and we'll go to the lake," I tried to reason with him. He sighed and held my shoulders as he kissed my head.

"I'll call the police station tonight to get some search divers, a police presence, and a couple of forensics guys out there with us," he said. I nodded, unable to do anything else.

"I'll see you in the morning," I said to him. I could tell he was reluctant to leave me alone, but he knew he didn't really have a choice.

27. When Ice Thaws

Aria only confirmed what I already knew, but talking to her helped me calm down and accept what I had actually already, deep down, known for months now. The next morning, I was a bit more somber when Liam picked me up accompanied by two squad cars. His parents and Bella were present as well. We went to the lake in silence. Liam was worried about me; especially since I was so quiet compared to the last time he saw me. We stood on the bridge and overlooked the lake as the policemen and divers searched for my dad. I crossed my arms as it felt like I held my breath as we waited. Liam stood next to me as we waited. Finally, there was movement.

"We found a car," they announced. I tried to prepare myself for what I knew was coming. As a crane pulled the familiar car out of the water, I knew that my premonitions had been right. I took a deep breath and turned away from the scene. I knew it was hard living without a mate. I told myself that he survived as long as he could. Longer than most, thanks to Aria.

"I'm sorry, Dani. Are you okay?" Liam asked as he turned his attention to me. I shook my head and ran my fingers through my hair, gripping the strands slightly.

"I knew this was coming, but it still breaks my heart," I answered softly. "But I'll be okay. He lived without his mate for 18 years after all. It's better that he's no longer suffering," I added. Liam took my hand in his. This was how it was supposed to be. I stepped into Liam and hugged him tightly. For once, I took comfort in the warmth of my mate to help me. Liam seemed happy that I was starting to rely on him more.

"Can we go? Please?" I asked quietly. He nodded before turning me away and leading me towards his car. As soon as I got in the car, I called my grandparents and let them know what was going on. Seeing the car was the only confirmation I needed. I didn't think I had the strength to identify the body. Liam took me to his house where we just sat in his room. I sighed and ran my fingers through my hair.

"Can you... distract me please?" I asked Liam in frustration when I felt my eyes start to water. He placed a hesitant hand on my back.

"When do you meet with Aria again?" He asked.

"I don't know. She pops in whenever she wants these days," I answered.

"Did you learn anything new?" He asked. I shrugged.

"Vision projection, weather manipulation, with all the usual powers," I answered quickly again.

"Dani," Liam asked making me look at him. As soon as I turned my head, his lips brushed against mine. I froze as his hand came around to my cheek, pulling me closer to him. I allowed it, too shocked to protest. But it helped. As soon as his lips touched mine, I couldn't think of anyone else but him. My hands came up on their own to tangle in his hair. I pushed him back against the bed, getting lost in his kiss. My lips started to wander on their own. Before I knew what was happening, I bit his neck.

It was like a splash of cold water hit me. I sat up quickly and covered my mouth with my hand. My skin graded against elongated canines, making me touch it with my finger.

They grew?

Liam sat up slowly as he stared at me in shock while holding his neck. We both stared at each other, unsure of what to say. I knew the meaning behind my actions, but they weren't my actions to take.

"You... you marked me?" Liam said out loud what we were both thinking. I marked him. In a normal situation, Liam would've been the one to mark me. Why did I mark him?

You're more dominant in this mating. You're stronger than him, but he can return the favor, Aria said in my mind. I gave a scoff before taking a breath.

"Aria says it's because I'm more dominant than you, but you can return the favor. But to be fair, it wasn't intentional," I replied. Liam chuckled and shook his head as his hand fell away from his neck. Past the slight smears of blood, a mark of a crescent moon laid near his collarbone. I couldn't help but to stare at it. It was so pretty.

"Is she telling me to mark you, too?" He asked, pulling me out of my own thoughts.

"Huh? Oh, probably," I said, snapping out of it.

"Is that what you want?" He asked. I quirked an eyebrow at him with a smirk. He was learning if he asked first.

"It only seems fair," I said as I pulled my hair off of my shoulder.

"You know what this means, right?" He asked again as he came closer. I smiled softly and moved closer to him as my arms went around his neck.

"It means that I'm your mate," I replied softly. He hesitated so I took the initiative to kiss him first this time. It was sweet, but easily heating up. This time, Liam flipped me onto my back. His arms propped him up to barely hover above me. He pulled away slightly breathless as he looked at me. Slowly, he brought his lips to my neck and placed soft kisses from my neck to my shoulder.after a breath, Liam's elongated canines pierced my skin making me gasp. A comfortable fire coursed through my veins instantly making me want Liam ten times more. Liam pulled away making my wound throb. I held it gently as blood trickled out of the punctures. I didn't seem to be healing like Liam did.

"I think I need a towel," I said awkwardly. Liam nodded and headed to the bathroom quickly before handing it to me. I pressed the towel against my neck before I sat up.

"I guess... your wolf really hasn't come yet," Liam said as he sat next to me.

"Five more days," I muttered. In five days, I would be 18 years old, and my wolf would come. In all honesty, I was scared for that day. I still wasn't eating meat the way I was supposed to be. I could keep down beef and pork most of the time, but chicken never stayed down. And if I could help it, I never ate meat willingly. I just hoped that when Sahria arrived she wouldn't destroy the whole town.

28. Sahria

When it was noticed, Liam's mark shocked everyone. The females typically didn't mark the males. Especially not the Alpha. I heard from Mya that he had a lot of explaining to do to his friends at school. The body in the lake was confirmed to be my father. My grandparents took care of the funeral preparations, so I wouldn't have to. After burying him with a proper funeral, it felt like I'd reached some closure on the chapter of my dad's life. I felt more towards Liam after we marked each other, and I could understand more where my father was coming from.

Finally, it was my birthday. Instead of a party, I was being taken deep into the woods of neutral territory. Alpha Connor, Liam, Luna Addie, and Aria were all there. Alpha Connor was leading the way. It would be their first time seeing Aria. I briefly wondered what form she would take, but seeing that this was a serious matter and not a showy one, I suspected her Welsh form. It was almost sunset when we finally got to the location. As soon as we stepped into the clearing, Aria appeared out of thin air.

"Dani... slow as always. Don't worry, that will change. You lucky you didn't start changing on the way here," Aria said as she stood there in front of us with her arms crossed. The Alpha Family all ententes their necks in a bow in a sign of acknowledgement and respect.

"Alpha family, go ahead and shift. Create a boarder near the tree line. It's almost time," Aria ordered. I caught myself rolling my eyes.

"You could be a little nicer. They are here to help after all," I retorted. Aria's eyes came back to me.

"We don't have the time," she answered. Liam stepped forward as Lina Addie and Alpha Connor turned to the tree line.

"Can I stay with her?" Liam asked shyly. Aria smirked at him.

"Dani may love you... But Sahria doesn't give a fuck right now," Aria answered. Liam's eyes widened before he jogged to the tree line too. Aria took my hands and made me sit in the middle of the field.

"Just breathe through the pain. It's going to hit soon," Aria said. As soon as I inhaled, a sharp pain made me stop in my tracks. It felt like the wind had been knocked out of me. Short breaths came out as my eyes watered.

"I'm... not... ready," I said through the breaths. Aria's hands squeezed mine gently, making me aware of her presence again.

"Just breathe," Aria reminded me. I tried, but it felt like my lungs were full of water. Something else snapped causing me to fall over. Aria's hands never left mine as she continued to tell me to breathe. The pain scorched my bones, leaving me in shock from the pain. My wide eyes leaked tears. I wanted to scream but I held it in. Everything was in pain. I felt like I'd been hit by a bus and then a high speed train. The pain felt like it continued for hours before I succumbed to the pain and blacked out.

***

I woke feeling sore and disoriented. I pushed up on my hands slowly with a groan. I felt a hand touch my arm as I was helped to a sitting position. The hand left tingles thought my arm. I reached out and hugged him close to me.

"Liam," I breathed. I was glad to see that he wasn't hurt. "How are you? She didn't hurt you, did she?" I asked as I pulled away to look at him. It was dark, but a light was almost immediately flipped on. I squinted at the sudden light an held my head gently. I had a headache. I focused my energy on making it go away before opening my eyes again.

"Sahria definitely hurt everyone in that clearing yesterday, but I told you I would protect them, and I did. Everyone is healed and fine," Aria said as she walked into the room. I sighed and ran my hand through my tangled hair.

"Yesterday?" I picked out. Aria smirked.

"Yes, you slept all day. You needed it. I actually expected you to sleep longer," Aria said.

"You've been here the whole time?" I asked curiously. Aria nodded.

"I didn't know if you would shift again, but I can go now," she said before disappearing. Liam, who was sitting next to me on the bed, put an arm around my waist.

"It's fine. We're all okay now," Liam tried to assure me. I tried to recall the events but I couldn't. Everything in Sahria's memory was blank to me. I sighed and held out my hand to Liam.

"Show me," I said, taking down my barrier. He hesitated before putting his hand in mine. Everything went black before the memory started.

Liam was watching me shift in the field. He wanted to help but he knew he would just get in the way. After I passed out, Liam couldn't stand by and watch anymore. He rushed forward in wolf form just as the shift was completed.

"I told you to stay back!" Aria yelled at him. My massive all white wolf launched at Liam before he could even turn around. Sahria caught his leg and snapped it making him whimper. Alpha Connor and Luna Addis's wolves immediately jumped into action.

"Don't interfere!" Aria tried yelling at them. The shock of her order made them freeze, making them easy targets. Sahria got her claws into Luna's hind leg. Alpha Connor stepped in to keep Sahria from hurting his mate. Sahria snapped at his front leg, but he stepped out of the way just in time. He moved to try to pin Sahria but she was bigger and stronger than him. Sahria's jaw clamped on his tail. Finally, Aria found an opening and pressed her hand against Sahria's head, causing her to collapse in a state of deep sleep. Aria healed everyone as Sahria slept in the middle of the clearing. After everyone was healed, they shifted back, putting their clothes back on. After another ten minutes, Sahria conceded, leaving me still sleeping and naked in the middle of the field.

I didn't even want to know what Liam was thinking about that, so I let go of his hand. I sighed and waited for my vision to dehaze.

"I'm sorry," I apologized. Liam's hand held my cheek as he kissed my head.

"We're all fine. I'm just glad that you're okay. Sahria is straight savage," Liam said. I sighed and rested my head against his as my hand held his.

"The worst is over," I breathed.

Oh how wrong I was...

29. Joint Pack Party

"Are you staying over the Alpha's house for dinner tonight," my grandpa asked. It was a common occurrence lately. Liam and I were practically inseparable these days. After I shifted on my birthday, Sahria stayed hidden, but she did provide some unseen perks. I healed faster by myself, I ran faster, all of my senses were incredibly enhanced, and even my demi-goddess powers came easier. The week following was intense training with Aria to test my limits. It was like a week straight of mental and CrossFit training. I was slightly taller, leaner, and even had a slightly more muscular build.

"Kind of. There's a party tonight that Liam is taking me to," I admitted. There was no reason to hide it from my grandparents, they were pretty cool with everything because they knew Aria was watching over me.

"Okay, be safe," he said. Mya came over and to get dressed with me. I wore a simple outfit of a cropped blue button-up blouse, skinny jeans, and ankle boots. Mya wore a cute crop top, an a-shaped skirt and blue jean jacket. Liam showed up and drove us to the party. The sun was done for the day, but the house was alive and electric when we pulled up.

"Who's party is this?" I asked as I got out of the car. Liam was quick to put his arm around me, and I didn't complain these days.

"Our neighboring pack invited the people from high school to their party. It's like a joint party that they have every year. Mainly it's for the potential mate and good connections," Liam explained. We went inside and Mya's mate was there in an instant to sweep her to the dance floor. Liam moved us into the kitchen where he got himself a drink. He handed me a virgin drink.

"No alcohol?" I asked curiously.

"Aria said no alcohol around a different pack," Liam muttered. I sighed but drank my drink anyway.

"Hey, aren't you that girl?" Someone asked, from behind me. I turned to see a guy with dark eyes and hair. He was fairly built. I opened myself to read his thoughts.

This is the girl everyone has been talking about. The Alpha's mate who dominates him. She fits the description of the girl Harvey saw in the clearing.

I smiled easily trying to be friendly. If I was going to figure this out, I needed to figure out who Harvey was.

"Yeah, I'm Liam's mate," I said. "Hey, my friend Harvey said he'd be here tonight. Do you know where I could find him?" I asked. I felt Liam's hand on my back.

Just wait. I need to figure something out, I said through mindlink to Liam. It was nice to finally be able to do that since Sahria appeared.

"Oh yeah, he's around here somewhere. Last I saw he was in the dining room on the couch," the guy said. I thanked him before heading to the dining room with Liam hot on my heels.

I need to handle this. Someone saw me shift in the clearing. Give me some space, I mindlinked to Liam. He sighed before stopping and going back to the kitchen. I went through everyone's thoughts and quickly found Harvey. I approached him unwavering. When he felt my presence, he turned and looked at me with wide eyes.

Shit! It's that white wolf. What is she doing here? Harvey thought to himself. I smiled at him easily.

"Harvey right? Could I talk to you in private for a moment?" I asked. He was quick to shake his head.

"No way! You're a freak!" He said quickly. My smile dropped and I got serious.

"You're making a scene. Follow without talking," I said using the persuasion power Aria taught me. His eyes were still wide but his mouth shut. I turned and went out to the backyard, knowing he would follow. When I was far enough out to not be disturbed, I stopped and turned to face Harvey.

"Now, you will answer my questions truthfully and quietly," I continued with my persuasion power. "What did you see the day I shifted?" I asked.

"Well, you shifted and almost tore the Alpha Family apart. The woman who was with you used magic or something to subdue you then she healed the entire Alpha Family. Who was she? Who the hell are you?" He asked.

"Who have you told?" I asked.

"Everyone I know. Our Alpha knows as well," he answered.

"What was his opinion?" I continued.

"He believes you to be a very powerful weapon. He wants you," Harvey answered against his will. I sighed and ran my hand through my hair. This wasn't good.

"Okay, you will go inside and forget I even came to this party. You will forget our conversation and the power I had over you," I said, using as much power as I could. He turned and walked back inside without another word.

We have to leave, I mind-linked to Liam and Maya.

Carson said he would take me home. You guys go ahead, Maya responded.

Meet me in the front, Liam replied to me. I walked around the house without going inside so I wouldn't be seen. Liam was already waiting for me out front.

"What happened?" He asked.

"Let's get in the car first," I said. He opened the passenger door for me before getting in the driver's side.

"What is going on?" He asked. I sighed, already trying to think of ways to fix the situation.

"That Harvey guy saw me shift in the woods and saw Sahria hurt you guys. He told everyone. Their Alpha views me as a powerful weapon now," I explained.

"How did Aria not sense him?" He asked confused.

"Sahria is extremely dangerous. All of Aria's attention was focused on her," I answered. "This pack may not know everything, but they know too much. It may not be a problem yet, but something tells me that it will be," I said.

"Let's go brainstorm with my mom. She may know what to do," he said before starting the car.

30. Complications

W e went straight to Liam's house and found Luna Addie in her office. As soon as we walked in, she could sense something was wrong. We quickly explained why was going on as we sat in the chairs in front of her desk. She bummed thoughtfully, twisting her rolling chair back and forth from behind her desk.

"Alpha Greg is an ally of ours. I think the best course of action would be to hold a meeting with him before things get out of hand," Luna Addie suggested. It sounded like a good idea. Just in case he may have been under the assumption that I hurt the Alpha family on purpose, it would be best to bring peace through a conversation.

"Who all would be at the meeting?" Liam asked curiously. I could sense his anxiousness.

"Your father, of course, me, maybe Beta Trevor, and Dani," Luna Addie answered.

"Why not me?" Liam asked, growing even more anxious.

"Your feelings for me as your mate might cause you to lash out, creating more of a problem," I answered, instantly understanding the Luna's reasoning.

"Correct, Dani," Luna Addie conformed.

"But I want to be there," Liam snapped.

"Look at you now. You can't even hold it together in front of your mother, there's no way I'm risking it at that meeting. Plus, I can take care of myself, so there's really nothing to worry about," I responded to him. He huffed and slumped down in his seat. The office door opened, averting our attention to Alpha Connor.

"Yes honey?" He asked, walking further into the room until he was standing next to Liam.

"We need to set a date for a meeting with Alpha Greg," Luna Addie explained.

"The date can't be on a new moon," Liam said quickly. I glared at him.

"Although you're right, that's not really for you to say," I said in frustration.

"They have to know, Dani," he replied.

"Your mom is already aware," I sighed as I pinched the bridge of my nose.

"Aware of what?" Alpha Connor asked. My hand fell away from my face as I looked at him.

"I'm the weakest during a new moon. I have to pull energy from nature on that day, or I get weak and dizzy. It was the reason I passed out in the woods when I first met Liam. The opposite goes for a full moon. Of course, I didn't know any better then," I explained.

"That shouldn't be a problem then. How about next week? It's supposed to be full," Alpha Connor suggested. I nodded in agreement. "I'll go make the call," he said before leaving the Luna's office.

"Sorry," Liam muttered sheepishly as he cast his eyes towards his lap.

"I also think you should stay at our house for the time being. I know you can handle yourself, but I don't want you inadvertently putting your grandparents in danger if anyone comes looking for you," Luna Addie said. Liam's thoughts were screaming at me. He was excited and immediately thought of finishing the mating process.

"This is not the time to be thinking about that, Liam," I exasperated as I glared at him. He blushed and tucked his chin into his chest to keep from looking at me. Luna Addie chuckled.

"I don't even want to know," she said as she shook her head. "Stay here for the night, you can borrow some of Bella's clothes for now. During the day tomorrow, I'll take you home to grab some of your things and explain your situation to the Wilders," Luna Addie added. I nodded. I knew she was right. It would be reckless to put my grandparents in danger when we didn't know the situation yet.

"Thank you," I smiled softly at her. We said our final words before Liam led me up the stairs to his room. His intentions didn't waiver far from his earlier thoughts.

"I'm not sleeping with you, Liam. And I'm not sleeping in your bed. There are plenty of guest rooms in this house," I said as soon as he closed the door behind us.

"You know, it kind of sucks that you can hear my every thought," he countered with a pout. I only chuckled and sat on his bed.

"I can't help that," I shrugged.

"And I can't help my thoughts. I want to be with you every second of the day and night, but I know you, so I refrain from being as possessive as I want to be. But our mate bond has grown stronger for me, and it was already strong from the start. I don't want you to ever leave my side, and I know how that sounds but I can't help it," he tried to explain. Being in his thoughts, I already knew how he felt. His thoughts were consumed with me. The mark on my neck felt hot suddenly.

"I get it. I really do, but in the situation that we're in right now, it's not safe. Getting caught up in each other right now will only blind us from everything else going on. One of us has to keep our eyes open," I responded. Liam's brain understood what I was saying, but his heart didn't. He lifted my chin and kissed me, releasing a gently sigh as he did so. My eyes closed on their own as my arms went around his neck, pulling him on top of me. It seemed that my heart didn't understand either. A knock on the door made us break away from each other. I quickly sat up and dangled my legs off of the edge of his bed.

"Come in," Liam said as he propped himself up on his arm. Bella came in unsurely, holding a few pairs of folded clothes in her hands.

"My mom told me to give this to you Dani," she said as she placed the clothes on the edge of the bed next to me. I thanked her before she left. I turned to Liam knowingly.

"A guest room, Liam," I said.

31. Alpha Greg

A week passed faster than I expected. After everything was explained to my grandparents, they were more than happy to send me to the Miller's house. I think they were just happy I would be spending time with my mate. I slept in the guest room every night, as promised, but in return, Liam spent way too much time in there too. It was like pulling teeth getting him to leave my room when it was time for bed. Similarly, it was hard to get him to leave for school, too. But while he was away, I used the time to practice my magic in the backyard. I could tell that I was getting stronger. I also used my time to eat meat. I still wasn't comfortable enough to do it at the dinner table, but red meat was easier to eat now.

Finally, the day of the meeting arrived. I waited with Alpha Connor and his Beta at the conference table, the analog clock ticking away the seconds in the silence almost as if it were mocking me. Liam took Bella and Lily to the mall to stay away from the house. It was a few minutes before Luna Addie walked into the room trailed by Alpha Greg and his Beta. I had my mental barriers down to keep a read on the room.

So that's the girl, Alpha Greg thought as his eyes landed on me. Everyone greeted each other as I stayed quiet. Alpha Greg and his Beta sat on the opposite side of the table and waited as Luna Addie sat next to me.

"There's been talk around you pack that you're interested in my son's mate. Mind telling me why?" Alpha Connor asked getting straight to the point.

She took out an entire Alpha Family in wolf form, who wouldn't want her? Alpha Greg thought to himself.

"It was a mere curiosity. I heard she was deadly in wolf form. I was just curious as to the exact extent," he said instead.

"Although that's true. I can't control her, so it would be useless to you. You may be the one getting hurt instead," I spoke up. Alpha Greg just laughed.

"I've heard other things as well from the high school aged kids in my pack. Apparently your pack talks as well. I heard she was only in school for a few months before dropping out for specialized training. A close friend of my daughters' also mentioned her as the girl with unexplainable powers and moon kissed eyes. How special is this specialized training?" he admitted.

"We do not run her training so we wouldn't be able to answer that," Luna Addie spoke up.

So it's true that she's being trained by the Moon Goddess then, Alpha Greg thought excitedly.

"How interesting indeed," he said.

"Being that Daniella is my son's mate, I find your curiosity worrisome," Alpha Connor said, lacing his fingers together under his chin.

"Is that so? Your son must have saved a nation in a past life to be as lucky as to be mates with this girl," Alpha Greg jokes. He was the only one who laughed.

"We are allies, are we not? Meaning I would help you if you were in trouble at a moment's notice, no questions asked. I would appreciate it if you did the same. No questions asked," Alpha Connor said sternly getting to his point.

"And would Daniella be a useful weapon to you or against you?" Alpha Greg countered.

"The Alpha Family is my family too," I spoke up.

"But if you can't control your wolf, who's to say you won't hurt them again?" He countered.

"That's for us to worry about," I replied easily. He thought to himself for a moment, going back and forth between getting involved and not before he stood with a sigh.

"I understand. Regardless, it was nice finally meeting you face to face," he said offering his hand for me to shake. I stood and took his hand, forgetting that my barriers were currently down. My vision blurred before a vision of him leading an attack on the pack appeared before me. While everyone else was fighting, he only had thoughts of slaughtering the Alpha family and taking me as a prize and a prisoner. The vision disappeared, leaving a fog in its place. Alpha Greg was staring at my eyes with excitement in his own.

"How very interesting indeed," he smirked before he left, tailed by his Beta. I sighed and pinched the bridge of my nose. After I heard his car drive away, I turned to Alpha Connor and Luna Addie.

"He saw my eyes. I forgot to put my barrier back, but I saw him. He's not going to let this go. He wants to kill everyone and take me as his own personal weapon," I explained. Alpha Connor stood before pinching the table. It cracked like a twig under his force.

"It's not your fault, Dani. Alpha Greg has always been somewhat greedy, and you're the equivalent of the Holy Grail to him," Luna Addie said, trying to make me feel better.

"What do we do? I can help some ways, but I can't save everyone if he goes through with his plan," I admitted.

"Don't worry, Dani. We'll be ready for him," Alpha Connor said, glaring at the door.

"Do you think it would be possible to keep this from Liam?" I asked. Luna Addie looked at me sympathetically before she shook her head.

"With extra training exercises for the warriors, a posted guard, and around the clock barrier patrols, he would be suspicious anyway. We're going to have to tell him, Dani," Luna Addie explained. I sighed and turned back to Alpha Connor.

"What about the alliance?" I asked him.

"For now, we'll pretend that we've let the issue go and get ready in secret. Also the kids can still interact, but that's just as to not cause any suspicion. He's expecting us to be completely unprepared, so we won't give him any reason to come at us any harder. If anyone outside of the warriors ask, we're beefing up boarder security due to rogues," Alpha Connor said, making his plans out loud. I nodded with a sigh.

Now to figure out how to tell Liam...

32. Because We're Mates

I paced as I waited for Liam to get home. I had been mulling over how to break the news to while keeping him from getting too angry or overprotective.i still hadn't figured it out when his room door opened. He looked at me expectantly.

"Well, how did it go?" He asked. I decided to just get to the point. It wouldn't do any good to beat around the bush.

"The conversation itself was fine, but he saw my eyes, and I saw his intentions in a vision because of it. He's planning an attack to take me, but before you overreact, your dad already has a plan together, and I'm staying at your house until all of this blows over," I explained quickly. A growl ripped through Liam's throat at he snarled at a spot on the ground.

"Over my dead body," he growled. I touched his arm gently in an attempt to calm him down.

"The warriors are going into training and boarder security will beef up with the excuse of rogues. I'm getting stronger every day, and I won't leave your side, okay? We just have to wait this out," I said quickly.

"What do you mean, you won't leave my side?" He asked curiously. I sighed and closed my eyes briefly.

"I... I won't leave your side. I know how anxious that makes you," I answered.

"But I still have to go to school," he reminded me.

"I know... I'll reenroll. Aria already said it was okay. I'll just be training with her after school," I caved. A small smile made its way to his face.

"And you have to stay in my room," he added, testing his luck. I sighed before I nodded.

"Fine. I'll stay in your room for a while," I agreed. He wrapped his arms around me and nuzzled his head into my shoulder.

"Deal," he said softly. I hesitated before wrapping my arms around his waist. Because of my dad, I knew how anxious a wolf could be without his mate. I didn't want to put Liam through that. Especially when things were about to get complicated because of me. I knew he wouldn't just let me leave, and this way, I could keep an eye on him as well. I knew Liam wasn't the type to stop and strategize when it came to me, his mate.

"I'll go to register tomorrow," I promised as I pulled away from him. He held on to my hand when I turned to leave.

"I'm just going to shower and change into pajamas. I'll be back," I assured him with a slight chuckle. He hesitated before letting go. I went to the guest room and did exactly as I said I would before going back to Liam's room. He was sitting on the edge of his bed waiting for me.

"Mom said dinner will be ready in half an hour," he said. I sat next to him with a sigh.

"I'm not all that hungry tonight," I replied before laying back to stare at the blank ceiling.

"I don't mean to be a pest to you, Dani. I know I can be a bit... overbearing sometimes, and I wish I could help it. I know, very well, that you don't really need me, but I can't help my urge to protect you," he admitted out loud. I turned my head to look at him. He was still sitting, facing the door, with his shoulders slouched. Defeat and helplessness rolled off of him in waves. I reached out and took his hand in mine gently.

"I know, Liam. I know that you can't help it. Why do you think I agreed to stay by your side? It certainly isn't for my sake. The only way you will feel at ease, is if you can keep an eye on me. But you are wrong about one thing. I do need you. I may not be a helpless lamb, and I may not need you to protect me physically every time, but I do need you... as my mate," I said softly. He looked at me with an overwhelming amount of love in his eyes as a gentle smile made its way to his face.

"You're smart, you know that?" He chuckled. I smiled before I kissed his cheek.

"I know," I joked.

"You should eat dinner tonight. You'll need your strength, and tonight's menu is spaghetti with meatballs. You still need to practice eating meat in front of people if you'll be going to school tomorrow. You can't skip it just because it'll be in front of people," he said. I sighed before I nodded. In all honesty, that shower woke up my appetite. He took my hand and led me down to the living room. Luna Addie and Alpha Connor smiled when they saw us.

"I was wondering if you were coming for dinner tonight. I set aside a portion without meat for you," Luna Addie smiled at me. I sit down as Liam set a plate in front of me and set a few meatballs on top.

"It's okay. I should start eating meat every chance I get. I don't want Sahria popping out at such a crucial time," I answered as they watched Liam sit next to me.

"I'm guessing you told him already," Alpha Connor said. I nodded.

"I told him everything, and... I'm reenrolling for school tomorrow," I explained.

"Any particular reason, Dani? Will Aria be okay with shortening your training?" Luna Addie asked. I nodded as I finished shallowing the bite I took.

"I know everything she had to teach me now so it's more about stamina and maintaining my physical and mental strength. Plus, Liam would probably throw a fit if I didn't stay by his side at this time. I don't want him being reckless," I replied. Alpha Connor chuckled.

"As long as everyone is okay with the arrangement, I don't see why not," he smiled happily.

"You're going to my school tomorrow?" Bella asked. I almost forgot that she was a sophomore there. I nodded.

"Although I will admit, I'm a little nervous about how everyone will receive me coming back," I admitted.

"If anyone has anything bad to say about you, they'll go through me first," Bella growled.

"And me too," Liam agreed. I laughed before taking another bite of my food. The rest of dinner was pleasant. I knew that school tomorrow would be less stressful with Liam and Bella by my side, but still, I would have to catch up on the schoolwork. Luckily, I was a wiz at speed reading and memorization now. My memory was photographic thanks to Aria. They seemed like trivial skills at the time but they were about to come in handy. It would've been wrong to cheat that way if the situation didn't call for it. I was actually looking forward to seeing Mya and the gang again in a casual setting. It'd been a while.

33. Back to School

L iam drove us to school the next day. Bella parted with us at the door, wishing me good luck while we continued on to the main office.

"Oh! Ms. Morrison, are you back?" The office lady asked. I remembered her from when I first enrolled at school. I nodded with a smile.

"Dani's schedule needs to mirror mine," Liam said. I resisted the urge to roll my eyes. He was taking the 'stick by my side' thing very literally, but I expected it. The office lady smiled warmly before typing on her computer.

"One moment," she said as she stood and grabbed something off of the printer. She came back and handed it to me while handing Liam another copy.

"There you are. It's good to see you again Dani," she said sincerely.

"You too," I smiled before Liam took my hand and led me into the main hallway. As soon as we stepped into the hallway, the atmosphere changed. People were trying to look at us without actually being obvious that they were looking at us. We stopped at my locker where books we're already placed inside.

"I had someone come put these here earlier this morning," Liam explained. I sighed and looked at my schedule before pulling out my books for the first few classes. Liam wasted no time taking them from me.

"Are you really going to go this far?" I asked with a sigh. He only smiled cheekily.

"Dani!" A girl's voice yelled from down the hall. I turned to see Mya charging towards me. My eyes widened as she continued charge. She wasn't slowing down. I didn't even bother bracing myself as she knocked me into the floor in a hug. I laughed along with her as we hugged laying there.

"Mya, it's like you're trying to hurt my mate. You know she won't fight you," Liam said to her as he pinched the bridge of his nose.

"I've missed you so much! Where have you been lately?" Mya asked, ignoring Liam.

"Under Liam-Watch practically 24-7. You know he's sensitive," I joked. I stood and offered Mya a hand up as well.

"Dani!" Liam said shocked. I chuckled and held his hand gently to make him feel better.

"Oh come on. You know it's true," I responded. Liam was too preoccupied staring at our hands to give any retort. He was like a little kid; the simplest things made him happy.

"I'm glad you're back," Mya giggled. I let go of Liam's hand to hug Mya again. Even though things had been busy, I wish I'd made more time for her. I considered her my best friend after all.

We walked to our first class where Liam made me sit next to him.I wasn't really interested in the lesson but more so in reading the thoughts of those around me. Turns out, no one was paying attention. Everyone had their own theory on my relationship with Liam and why I was back. A couple of people even speculated that I might be pregnant. That theory was laughable. As slow as I was taking things with Liam, that probably wouldn't happen for a long time.

Thankfully, the day was passing pretty quickly. Before I knew it, it was time for lunch. Luna Addie packed a lunch for me since I was on a "special" diet of reintroducing meats. I sat at the lunch table next to Mya like I did before. Liam wasted no time pouting about it.

"You promised to stay by my side," he whined.

"Then sit next to me," I offered. He hesitated before he finally sat down. Slowly, the table filled up with the usuals. Kaden smiled at me when he took his seat.

"I heard the rumor but I didn't think it was actually true. Welcome back, Dani," Kaden said to me. I smiled back to him with a light chuckle.

"Thanks," I replied.

"Are you eating meat now?" Mya asked in shock. I shrugged as I finished chewing my food.

"Mostly," I answered.

"So I guess the shifting wolf in the woods was you," a new but familiar voice joined us. Sophia took her seat before picking up my utensils.

"The next pack over has this rumor about a shifting wolf almost taking out the entire Alpha Family. I guess they were talking about you," Sophia said.

"Not true. Bella and Lily weren't there," Liam corrected her.

"Wait seriously?!" Kaden asked. I only shrugged.

"You attacked the Alpha Family and didn't get taken down immediately?!" He asked. I shrugged.

"She didn't know she was doing it. Her wolf has a completely different conscious than Dani," Liam explained.

"That's insane," Mya put in her two cents.

"Well, it's not really up to me," I added.

"Weird till the end, huh?" Sophia said, finally talking again. I smiled sarcastically and resisted the urge to flip her the finger. The emotions between us still weren't great, but it was understandable.

"Anyway, that Alpha is after her now and he's not past destroying the whole pack to get to her," Liam said.

"Is she really worth all of that?" Sophia asked.

"If you knew half of what she could do, you would understand. She's basically walking pack protection. He's not the only one who would kill to get his hands on her," Liam explained.

"So I guess it's a good thing that she's your mate," Kaden said. Liam nodded as he ate his food.

"That's the only way we even knew what was going on. Otherwise, we'd be in the dark. Needless to say, this stays in the pack," Liam explained. I could already see Sophia plotting to get rid of me. Her hands weren't busy enough with her paralyzed mate?

"You already have your mate and I have mine. What do you gain by getting rid of me?" I called her out.

"You could've healed him more. Why did you stop?" She pushed back.

"The Moon Goddess told me to," I answered easily. "Your hands were too idle. Her words, not mine," I added. She pointed her glare at me before it shifted to the table. She wouldn't get her way that easily.

34. Hen Amongst Roosters

"We're home!" I yelled across the house as we walked through the door. Liam was still fuming about Sophia planning to tell the other pack about me.

"How was your first day back?" Luna asked as we came into the kitchen. She looked between the two of us before she turned the water off and leaned on the counter.

"What happened?" She asked instinctively.

"Sophia is out for blood," Liam muttered as he rolled his eyes. Luna Addie sighed as she took her dish gloves off and came around the counter.

"When will that girl ever learn?" Luna Addie said mostly to herself. "If it's come to the, we'll have her and her mate quarantined. I won't have her risking this pack's safety for a petty vendetta," Luna Addie explained. Liam nodded in agreement. To be completely honest, I wanted to use her to test my abilities. That seemed like a more fitting punishment, but I knew that was just me being petty as well.

"Dani has training this afternoon. We'll be a little late to dinner," Liam said as he grabbed an apple from the fruit bowl. Luna Addie acknowledged him before going back to the dishes.

"Just be careful. It'll be her first time training with the pack. We don't need Sahria coming out unnecessarily," Luna Addie gave her last bit of advice before we went upstairs. Liam has the rest of my things brought to his room while we were at school, so we just went straight to his room.

"Most of your clothes should be in the closet but I think your workout gear is in this dresser," he said. I rummaged through the clothes until I found a suitable outfit and set it on the bed. Liam eyed the clothes warily.

"Don't you have something more... conservative?" He asked. I rolled my eyes as I turned to face him.

"No, I don't. It's too hot for winter clothes, Liam. Would you like me to pass out from heat exhaustion?" I asked sarcastically. He sighed and looked at the clothes on the bed before he picked out a pair of basketball shorts and a plain t-shirt.

"I'll change in the bathroom, you can change here," he changed the subject before he walked quickly, closing the door behind him. I stripped off my school clothes and changed my regular bra to a sports bra. I pulled on the spandex type shorts before grabbing the pink athletic top. It was in the style of a very fitted tank top.

"I'm not letting you go out there with those shorts," I heard Liam say from behind me. I stopped with the top still in my hands and turned to face him.

"Letting me?" I picked out as I raised an eyebrow at him. He should know better than to use controlling words on me. I paused as I looked at the shirt in my hands.

"Wait a minute. You came out early on purpose, didn't you?" I asked suddenly. His cheeks turned bright red as he looked away from me.

"N-No I didn't," he said quickly. I chuckled and set the shirt on the bed before taking a step closer to him.

"I don't even have to read you to tell that was a lie. But it's fine for you to look. I'm your mate anyway," I said before picking my shirt up again and putting it on this time.

"I really wish you would wear different shorts," Liam pleaded. I smirked before I grabbed a light athletic jacket and zipped it halfway. Even with the jacket, my figure came through clearly. I threw my tennis shoes on before heading towards the door.

"You can stay here if you're just going to mope. I don't want to be late," I said before opening the door. Liam sighed heavily before he followed behind me. We drove out to the practice field before we headed towards the waiting crowd. Alpha Connor was already standing at the head of the crowd. He smiled when he sat us.

"Today's training will incorporate Liam's mate, and our secret weapon, Dani," he explained as we stood beside him. I heard a few scoffs and protests but I was expecting it. The women didn't really take part in the fighting unless it was absolutely necessary.

"How do you expect us to fight and keep that little girl out of trouble at the same time," someone from the crowd said. I smirked and took a step forward.

"How about this? Bring out your best fighter. I guarantee he won't be able to even scratch me. If I'm wrong, I'll stay out of it," I promised. Liam held my arm gently as if to tell me he didn't agree. I already know that.

"No way, you should start with a less seasoned warrior if you don't want to get hurt," the guy said from the crowd again. I chuckled as the smirk reappeared in my face.

"I suggested the strongest to even the playing field for your side," I explained. They all hesitated before the guy who was talking finally stepped out of the crowd and came to stand in front of me.

"Fine. I'll even be a gentleman and let you go shift in the tree line first," he said.

"No thanks. I don't t shift on command. Plus, she's more dangerous to all of you than I am," I declined.

"So do I shift?" He asked confused. I shrugged.

"Whatever form you feel the strongest in," I offered. He walked towards the tree line before coming back as a wolf. I could tell Liam didn't like this at all, but he knew better than to try and stop me. I took a deep breath and opened myself for his thoughts without opening my vision channel as I closed my eyes.

"Umm... Miss you might want to open your eyes. The match is about to start," someone else from the crowd called out.

"I'm aware. It's easier this way," I called back. It got dead silent as Liam looked between the two of us nervously.

"Begin," he commanded.

35. Red Moon

I t wasn't that hard to avoid the wolf I was fighting. Because I was in his head, I knew his every move before he made it. He couldn't touch me. I dodged ever single one of his advances. When I started to get bored, I simply touched his arm and converted energy through my hands to make him sleep. Not once did I open my eyes. It was probably a little too easy. I never even took my jacket off. The crowd was silent as they watched their comrade snore peacefully on the ground.

"Any more questions?" Alpha Connor said smugly. I could sense he was proud as I opened my eyes and went to stand by Liam. A lot of them were stunned, some impressed, and others were scared. It was to be expected. The others began training as the guy I fought finally began to come to his senses. He shot up quick, no longer in wolf form and looked around confused.

"What happened?" He asked quickly. I shrugged as I smirked.

"You got completely embarrassed; that's what happened. Nice going Waylon. You should know what you're up against before you start running your mouth," Liam explained. I smirked at Waylon as he stretched.

"I guess having you around can counter having you around," Waylon said smartly.

"Hey," Liam growled in warning. Waylon only chuckled as he pat a hand on Liam's shoulder.

"Relax, it's a joke. Of course we would protect our next Luna. It goes without saying," Waylon clarified.

***

"What happens during a red moon?" I asked Aria. It had been a few weeks and nothing had happened, but we still continued to train. It was a rare time I had with Aria. She hadn't been around in physical form as of late. She showed up suddenly to warn me of the upcoming red moon.

"Nothing really for other wolves, but for you, it's when you're most dangerous. One of two things will happen: Sahria will take over your human form and all your powers with it, or you'll be able to stay conscious if you shift. It really depends on what form your in when the moon hits," Aria explained.

"How long does it last?" I asked.

"Until the moon goes back to its original form and color. Sometimes, it's a day, sometimes two," she shrugged.

"But I can't even control my shift as it is," I sighed as I laid back on the bed. Liam was talking to his dad in his office, which is probably why Aria suddenly appeared.

"You would have to rile Sahria up in order to shift. Once that happens, you can control both forms and Sahria will sleep, but you have to be careful because if you don't shift before the red moon appears, Sahria will be the one in control of both forms. And don't think she doesn't know how to use your powers, she does. Everything you're conscious of, she is too," Aria explained. I sighed and rubbed my forehead with my hand.

"When is the red moon?" I asked, already exhausted. Aria hesitated.

"It's tonight," she answered softly. I shot up and stared at her.

"And you're only telling me this now?" I asked. She shrugged.

"I forgot," she said. I looked out the window. The sun was already begin-ning to set. I stood quickly before I ran out of the room. I went down the stairs and threw open the door of the Alpha's study.

"We've got a problem," I said quickly. I knew I was being rude by interrupt-ing them, but this was an emergency. Just as I said that, a siren blared.

We were under attack.

Liam and Alpha Connor shot up at the same time and headed towards me. I held my hands out to stop them as I blocked the doorway.

"Believe it or not, my problem is bigger than that," I said. They looked at me confused and worried.

"If I don't figure out a way to pull Sahria out to shift right now, she'll have control over my body and powers until the next moon," I explained quickly. They still looked confused. I sighed before I grabbed Liam's arm.

"Just take me somewhere isolated and get her mad. We don't have time," I said in a rush as I dragged him towards the front door.

"You two go do that. I'll handle the attack," Alpha Connor said before he ran out the back. Liam ran ahead of me and I followed him into the tree line. After a while of running, we stopped, still covered by trees.

"Okay, how do I get her mad?" He asked.

"You're our mate, surely you can think of something?" I yelled at him. I was scared. Scared of why Sahria would do while we were already under attack.

"Okay, um, you're ugly," Liam tried. I deadpanned to him as I crossed my arms.

"It needs to sound like you mean it. More," I said. He winced like he wasn't comfortable doing it.

"I know you don't mean it. I need you to do this, please? We're almost out of time," I begged as my eyes watched the sunset.

"Okay. I never really loved you. I don't want you as a mate. I wish I never met you," he yelled. I felt my legs snap, bringing me to my knees as I cringed and bit my lip to keep myself from yelling from the pain.

"More," I breathed when I realized that he stopped.

"I still love Sophia and I'm seeing her behind your back," he said quickly. That was it. That was the final nail in the coffin. I collapsed so I was on my hands and knees now as I gasped for breaths.

"Run," I choked out to Liam before I completely lost consciousness.

36. The Battle

When I came to, I realized my body wasn't on the ground anymore. I was growling and had Liam pines against a tree. Sahria must have gone after him after I shifted. I stopped growling and stepped back before I focused on slowing my heart rate and shifting back. When I opened my eyes, Liam was staring at me in shock.

"Dani... you literally look like you're on fire," Liam breathed. I looked at my arms to see that I was covered in a red glow.

"Your eyes," Liam said subconsciously. I didn't have time to ask him about it. Enemy wolves came towards us, growling from the tree line. The growling stopped when I turned to face them. They were looking at my eyes. I held a hand out and called out a hush of wind. It was more powerful than anything I'd done before. They cowered back before turning and running away.

"We need to go help you dad," I said quickly. Liam handed me an extra pair of clothes which I tossed on before I began running to where the action was. When we reached the field, wolves were going for each other's throats. I looked around as I tried to think up a plan. I couldn't do a mass attack because it would hurt our pack as well. I would just have to go through them one by one until they decided to retreat. I ran towards the first pair of fighting wolves and managed to touch the enemy wolf. I inflicted pain before I moved out of the way as the wolf collapsed. A long, deep gash run up its side.

I looked at my hands briefly. I would have to be careful. My power was magnified one hundred percent of not more. I ran through the fighting wolves one at a time as I inflicted pain through my fingers to each of the enemy wolves. I could see Liam and Alpha Connor also fighting in the distance. The wolf Alpha Connor was fighting was Alpha Greg. If we could defeat him, we could end this whole thing. I ran towards them as I continued to help our pack with the wolves they were fighting. When I finally reached the alphas, they were circling each other again to break from fighting. I painted softly as I watched them.

"Alpha Connor, Do you mind if I take this one? It is me he wants, after all," I asked. Alpha Connor nodded and gave me permission in his mind before he backed up. I stepped forward as I took a breath.

She glows now? Even dead, I bet she'd make a perfect nightlight, Alpha Greg thought.

"I don't think I'd still glow if I died," I said out loud. He growled before he charged at me. He didn't like the fact that I was in his head. Of course, I anticipated that and quickly dodged his attacked. While his back was turned, I grazed my fingers on his hind leg and inflicted pain. He helped as he turned away from me quickly. His back leg was bleeding, but he only seemed to be more on the defense. He continued to come at me while trying to avoid my hands. He was a fast learner. Everything I could do was through touch. He actually had a chance of winning this way. I had to think of something. An idea popped into my head as he lunged at me again. I quickly put a glamour on myself so he would see me hurt and unable to continue. I sat on the floor as I heard him snicker. He lunged for the final kill shot. When he did, I grabbed him around the throat and put everything I could into inflicting pain on him. A deep cut circled where my hands were as blood gushed out. The blood shined from the glow of the moon. A howl sounded before the enemy wolves began to flee. I pulled my blood-soaked hairs away from the dead alpha as I sighed. His body collapsed to the ground as his body lay lifeless. I felt arms go around me as Liam sighed near my ear.

"You scared me to death! I thought he actually hurt you. And you know I didn't mean all that earlier right? I was just trying to make Sahria mad," he said quickly. I chuckled and relaxed into his side.

"I know," I smiled. We left as Alpha Connor took care of the body. When I got inside the house, I went straight to the bathroom and began washing the blood from my hands. I scrubbed until it was all gone. I splashed water on my face before looking at myself in the mirror. The red glow was still very noticeable, but what caught my attention was my eyes. They were tiny replicas of the red moon outside. My pupil was completely gone like it was when I was having a vision. My appearance reminded me a lot of Aria in her depicted form, just with a red glow instead of a white one. I could only stare at myself.

"Dani, are you okay?" Liam asked as he wrapped his arms around my waist from behind me.

"I look... unreal," I said slowly. It was the truth. Even with my powers, I always felt grounded by the fact that I was still a human being, but right now, the fact that I was still human wasn't believable.

"Come on," Liam said as he pulled me out of the bathroom. He took me to the dining room where Luna Addie was setting the last dish on the table.

"Eat up! You've all had a long day," she smiled at us. The whole family was here: Bella, Lily, Luna Addie, Alpha Connor, And even my grandparents were here. I smiled at them sheepishly. I was happy to see them, but I was ashamed of how I appeared at the moment. I think it caught everyone off guard as they stared st me.

"I-I'm actually not that hungry tonight," I lied as I stood before retreating to Liam's room quickly. I sighed as I closed the door behind me. I was actually starving, but the looks were a little unnerving. Liam entered the room after I moved towards the bed. I looked at him in surprise when I saw the plates in his hands.

"You should still eat. I know you're a little... uncomfortable right now with your look, but you shouldn't starve because of it," he explained. I thanked him before I dug in.

37. We Should Be Mates

After Alpha Greg's mistake, no one bothered the pack or me, again. Even Sophia kept her mouth shut around me after she heard what I did. I ended up staying with Liam even though the danger passed. I'd gotten so comfortable with him, and I would've ended up staying with him anyway. My grandparents completely understood, but they still can to visit me. I even stayed in school until the year ended. Summer came faster than I was expecting. Before I knew it, we were graduating. The event made me think about what I wanted to do with my life. I knew I would have to stay and become the next Luna, but that wasn't all I wanted out of life. Now to just figure out how to tell Liam that. Behind his back, I applied to a few colleges across the country. I was waiting in our room for him after dinner to break the news.

"Why are you standing there?" Liam chuckled as he came back to our room from a meeting. I sighed and rubbed my hands together for the sake of something to do.

"I want to go to college. I applied to colleges all over the country and got accepted to a few of them," I said quickly. I thought it would be better to just rip the bandaid off. Liam froze as he stared at me.

"We don't get the luxury of going to college; especially future Alphas and Luna's. My dad is preparing to pass on his title to me soon. I can't leave and neither can you," he said seriously.

"Who said we can't go to college? Where is it written?" I retorted. He scoffed.

"It may have been a little different if you were a normal wolf and you weren't fated to become a Luna, but you can't even control your wolf as well as others can! There are so many rules that you, specifically, have to follow. If you leave pack grounds, you won't have an ally. You can't tell anyone about your connection with Aria or the fact that you're even a wolf. What if there's another red moon? Who's going to help you keep control? I can't leave and go with you, and no one else can aggravate Sahria. Plus, how would you explain the fact that you literally glow red. What if you get stuck in the city during a new moon and can't recharge? What if Sahria ends up welcoming out on her own? What if someone figures out what you are and sends you off to a lab?" He ranted.

These were all things I had not thought about. Ever since I was with my dad, I thought college was obviously in the cards for me. I guess I should've completely thought through all the changes I'd gone through in the last year. I looked towards the floor. I wasn't going to lie; I was disappointed, but more so because everything Liam said was valid. I was the last person who should've been thinking about leaving for college. I was a walking risk, a weapon, a blessing and a curse. Liam sighed and pulled me into a hug.

"I don't mean to be harsh, Dani, but this is the only way I can get you to seriously think about what you are in this world. You can't change your connection to Aria, and I understand it can be a burden sometimes, but there's nothing you can do to change that. The sooner you accept that, the easier your life will get," he said gently.

"I get it," I said softly.

"But honestly, now that everything has calmed down, I wanted to talk to you about completing our mate bond," he said hesitantly. I sighed and ran my fingers through my hair.

"It's not that I don't accept you, because I do, but I just... haven't thought about going there yet. With everything that happened, I never thought about it. Plus, isn't it like a hundred percent guarantee that if we do, I'll get pregnant. I don't know what exactly will be passed down if I have children, and that bothers me," I said honestly.

"Can't you ask Aria?" He asked. I sighed and sat down.

"She doesn't know either. I'm the first of female my kind," I answered.

"So you never want to complete our mating?" He asked.

"For now, no, but it's not forever. Plus, I'm a virgin. I just don't want to go there yet in general. You on the other hand..." I trailed off. He rolled his eyes at me.

"I thought we were dropping that?" He asked, referring to Sophia. I shrugged.

"I did drop it, but facts are facts. You're... experienced in that area. You probably already know what you like and what you don't like. I don't like the pressure of those expectations," I worded carefully. He sighed before he sat next to me and took my hands in his.

"As long as it's you, I'll be satisfied," he said. I pretended to gag.

"Oh my god, that was so cringeworthy. Never say that again," I said seriously as I took my hands out of his to stand up.

"I was being completely honest," he tried to defend himself. I smirked before I pet his head teasingly.

"That's what made it worse," I joked. He grabbed my arm and pulled me on to his lap.

"We'll have to finish it at some point," he said seriously. I raised an eyebrow as I craned my neck to look at him.

"You should know better than to rush me by now," I reminded him. He sighed and leaned his hands back on the bed.

"I know you're stubborn and like things to go your way. I know you don't technically need me. I know you like to control... well everything, but I can't wait forever. Even marked, without completing the process, I can go feral," he said. I sighed and stood up again.

"I'll think about it," I promised before I went to find Luna Addie for something to do.

Epilogue

----

* Two years later...*

"I'd like you all to welcome your new Alpha: Alpha Liam," Alpha Connor announces. It had been two years since we graduated high school. Bella has also graduated and Liam was officially becoming Alpha. I'd stayed with the Millers family in their home while I studied online for college. I wanted an education, at least, and since I couldn't leave the pack, I compromised. Liam and I had completed the mating process a year prior, and we'd been doing it ever since. Liam's initiation didn't take long. It was the afterparty I was worried about. I hadn't been up for socializing lately, but I had my duties as a mate, and the new Luna.

"Congratulations Luna Dani! How much tome do you have left?" Maya asked when she finally found me in the crowd.

"Two more months and I'll finally be done," I sighed with my hands holding my lower back. Her hand went to my stomach as she smiled widely. I was seven months pregnant and completely exhausted. Initially, I didn't get pregnant the first few times we mated, but I knew it was bound to happen, and it did. I'd gotten better at keeping Sahria in check on my own, but when I got pregnant, she always stayed away. Aria didn't come around as often because I didn't need her as much these days. By this point, I'd gotten a handle on my powers and what I needed to do to survive. But because of the battle with Alpha Greg, I didn't need to hide who I was anymore. My reputation proceeded me.

"Dani," Liam called to me as he smiled. He jogged over to me and kissed me lightly. "You don't have to be out here. I know you're probably tired," he said as his hand rested on my stomach.

"More like exhausted," I chuckled.

"Go inside and rest," he said. I nodded before I wobbled back to the house and to our room. I sat on the bed with a sigh and used the toe of my feet to get my shoes off. There was no way I'd be able to reach my feet in my condition.

"How are you feeling these days?" a familiar voice asked. I looked over in shock to see Aria sitting on the chair of my vanity.

"Aria," I said. She chuckled.

"Duh," she smirked.

"What are you doing here?" I asked. She sighed before she stood and came to sit next to me on the bed.

"I came to say goodbye," she admitted. I looked at her confused. I didn't understand.

"Goodbye?" I asked. She nodded as she looked at her lap.

"Yup. You and I won't see each other for a while. I have nothing left to teach you. Everything else, you'll have to figure out on your own. I'll be gone for a long time. But I'll be back eventually," she promised.

"If you're leaving, why would you come back?" I asked, even more confused than I already was. She smiled lightly and placed a hand on my stomach.

"I'll be back to help teach this one when she's old enough," she explained. My jaw dropped.

"I thought you didn't know if my powers would be passed on?" I asked.

"I don't know for sure. But I'm going to assume that she'll have something. It would be more surprising if she didn't," Aria explained.

"Why didn't you tell me this earlier?" I asked. She gave me a knowing look.

"Would you have completed your mating process with Liam if I told you?" She asked. I blushed and looked at my stomach. The answer was a strong 'no'. She chuckled.

"That's what I thought. But now that you have, are you happy?" She asked. I smiled lightly as I nodded.

"Extremely," I admitted. She stood with a sigh.

"Good. Then I'll see you in a decade or so," she winked at me before she vanished into thin air.

www.ingramcontent.com/pod-product-compliance
Lightning Source LLC
Chambersburg PA
CBHW070354200726